Writing in a hybrid form, Leslie Li sear[...] as she transitions from one mode to a[...] grand acts (both laudable and shameful) power *The Forest for the Trees*. The narrative compresses three generations of family history into one difficult year in the life of a Chinese-American family, whose members are struggling to locate themselves amid competing and conflicting cultural, economic, religious, and personal value systems.

—Debra Spark, author of *Discipline*

The Forest for the Trees is a genre-bending treat, both playful and hard-hitting, funny and insightful. Leslie Li's characters wrestle with painful questions of loyalty—to each other, to previous generations, to nations and codes of conduct—while they garden and tap dance and give the exact wrong performance at a birthday dinner. This is a multigenerational family drama neatly tucked inside a swift-moving, delightful novel inside a movie inside a novel.

—Caitlin Horrocks, author of *Life Among the Terranauts*

This book was such an intriguing read—I identified with all of the characters. The story speaks volumes about Chinese Immigrants landing on new soil, reluctant to embrace their new environment. It mirrors the many family dynamics I grew up with as an American-born, first-generation child watching my friends' immigrant parents slowly assimilating through their children who were born in the landed country. The scene with Nai-nai yelling to stop the car came right out of my own experience. Just like Nai-nai, my mother yelled at the top of her lungs to stop the car in the middle of our Seattle neighborhood when she saw—growing wild, bountiful and free—gow gay!!! Instead of the Land of the Gold Mountain (Gim San), for her, America could have been the Land of Abundant Gow Gay! A thoroughly enjoyable read.   —Lori Tan Chinn, actor, *Kung Fu Panda 4* and *Awkwafina Is Hangin' With Grandma*

the forest for the trees

the forest for
the trees

leslie li

black lawrence press

Black Lawrence Press

Executive Editor: Diane Goettel
Book Cover and Interior Design: Zoe Norvell

ISBN: 978-1-62557-151-9

Published 2024 by Black Lawrence Press.
Printed in the United States.

To the
memory of
Madame D.,
francophile,
who set
the pen
in my hand.

ailanthus altissima

Known Hazards:

The plant is possibly poisonous.
Male flowers have potentially
allergenic pollen. The leaves are
toxic to domestic animals. Gardeners
who fell the tree may suffer
rashes. The odor of the foliage is
intensely disagreeable and can
cause headache and nausea,
rhinitis and conjunctivitis. The
pollen can cause hay fever.

Article in the Arts & Culture section of a major New York City
newspaper, September 20, 2007:

Author Lucinda Wu was arrested for arson and grave robbery at Running Brook Cemetery, Westchester County. After explaining that she was "grave gifting"—not grave robbing—to honor the memory of her father at whose gravesite the "sacrificial offerings" were being made, the charges against her were dropped and personal effects confiscated by the police—a partially burned screenplay and a piece of jade—were returned to her. Wu's debut novel Ailanthus Altissima *was shortlisted for the New York Book Critics' Award and has been adapted as* Face To Face, *a feature film scheduled for release in early October.*

Telephone conversation between Lucinda and her publicist Phoebe, September 21, 2007:

Lucinda (looks at phone caller ID, groans softly, answers): Good morning, Phoebe.

Phoebe: What a BRILLIANT stratagem! *Succès de scandale.*

Lucinda: If you're referring to my arrest, it's not what I had intended.

Phoebe: That's what makes it so brilliant. If you meant for it to happen, if you'd planned it out carefully, it wouldn't have. Congratulations. You couldn't BUY better publicity.

Lucinda: Unless I'd been convicted. As a felon. On two counts.

Phoebe: Bad publicity is a lot better than no publicity. It's often better than good publicity. Even GREAT publicity. Actually, it IS great publicity. Guess where AA is on Amazon?

Lucinda: I take it you don't mean Alcoholics Anonymous.

Phoebe: A HORRIBLE title, Lucinda. Ailanthus Altissima. No one knows what it MEANS. Or can even pronounce it.

Lucinda: The subtitle says it all.

Phoebe: I know you fought your publisher tooth and nail to keep it, but you'd have twice the readership if you'd simply called it *Tree of Heaven*. Number 5 on Amazon. After ONE DAY. All the way up from number 74. And all because of that article. Which, by the way, has been picked up by two news services and one literary magazine. With more to come. Newspapers. Magazines. Bloggers. Podcasts. People I've PLEADED with to interview you or write a review of AA —now they're BEGGING me for the chance. Television. PRIME TIME TV. The Olive Winters Show. The Chuck Rowe Hour. Even the timing—right before *Face to Face* hits the theaters—couldn't be better.

Lucinda: Do they want to interview Lucinda Wu the writer. Or Lucinda Wu the arsonist/grave robber.

Phoebe: This is national media we're talking about. National television. The crème de la crème. You've risen to the TOP!

Lucinda: Of what.

Phoebe: Cancel any engagements you have for the next two, no three, weeks. You're completely booked.

Lucinda: I'm grateful to you, Phoebe, for all your good work, but you're not answering my questions.

Phoebe: Blue.

Lucinda: What?

Phoebe: For your television appearances. Wear blue. No stripes. A solid color. Nothing fussy. Television is RUTHLESS. It makes you look 10, 15 pounds heavier. But that's not a problem you have to worry about. And a good makeup department will make you look 10 years younger.

Lucinda: (stifling a snort) Maybe a breast augmentation is in order.

Phoebe: (pause) Just wear a molded bra. Doesn't have to be padded. And make sure you mention *Face to Face*—how unusual, no, INCREDIBLE, it is for a first novel to be made into a Hollywood movie. And how's this for an idea. Tell them your run-in with the police has given you an idea for your next book. A ghost story. Ghost stories are really hot right now. Catch the wave. You're honoring your father's memory by burying the jade cicada in his grave. His spirit rises from the dead and speaks through it—through the "tongue of jade," as you call it in AA.

Lucinda: Phoebe, you amaze me. Here I thought you were my publicist and you're acting as though you're my publisher.

Phoebe: I'm not telling you what to write. I'm merely telling you what will SELL. When marketing speaks, editorial listens. I'm a seasoned professional, and the fact that you pulled off the publicity stunt of the decade, of the CENTURY… I'd have given my eye teeth to come up with a ploy like that. My EYE TEETH, Lucinda. And you did it UNWITTINGLY. I mean, except for incest or child pornography, what's more lurid than grave robbing!

(Click)

Phoebe: Lucinda?

ailanthus altissima

(tree of heaven)

a novel

BY

LUCINDA WU

When she was a child, her favorite TV show was *Winky Dink and You*. The program featured a star-headed cartoon character with a squeaky voice. To watch the program, viewers had to buy Winky's Magic Window and Magic Crayons. The Magic Window was a sheet of transparent blue vinyl that adhered to the screen by virtue of static electricity. By connecting the dots (which appeared one by one on the television screen and similarly and sequentially disappeared from it) with a Magic Crayon, the viewer created a simple image—a Magic Picture. A bridge so that Winky could cross a river. An axe so he could chop down a tree. A cage so he could trap a man-eating lion. Denise loved *Winky Dink and You* because it invited—it *required* —her participation. Children who hadn't bought the Magic Screen and the Magic Crayons were missing out on Winky's fantastic adventures. They couldn't see the bridge, the axe, the lion's cage. Only an empty space on their TV screen. A space where important events were happening, that they couldn't see, from which they were excluded. But Denise could see them. What's more, she created them. She was part of Winky's magical world.

Years later, when the ultimatum came down from on high—no television on weekdays and one hour each day of the weekend—Denise found a substitute. Rather, the substitute found her. The solution to her father's weekday television ban was hiding in plain sight. The large window next to her bed: that became her new TV screen. The venetian blinds that covered the window, slats closed at bedtime: that was now her Magic Window. The sumac tree outside the window: that was her set of Magic Crayons. The shadows its branches cast onto the venetian blinds: they were the Magic Pictures.

Even before her father's edict, even before she connected *Winky Dink and You* to her current problem as its solution, the last vision Denise had before falling asleep at night was whatever image the hands of the sumac tree drew on the venetian blinds, whatever movie reel was spooling between her hypnogogic mind and the *ailanthus altissima*. Where before the visions were vague, amorphous, now that her father had spoken, the Magic Pictures drawn by her Magic Crayons on her Magic Window were as vivid and detailed as if she were sitting in a real movie theater watching a real movie—not lying in bed, her eyelids closing, drifting somewhere between sleep and wakefulness. But no matter how perfectly delineated or animated those images were, all of them were inconsequential, random, meaningless. They never constituted a story. Not until Prudence ran off and eloped.

face to face

a screenplay
by Lucinda Wu

Based on the novel
Ailanthus Altissima by Lucinda Wu

Lucinda Wu
181 Waverly Place
New York, NY
(212) - - -   - - - -

BLACK SCREEN
The SOUND of CICADAS BUZZING.
FADE IN:

EXT. A NEW YORK CITY SUBURB, 1959 — NIGHT

We approach a TUDOR-STYLE HOUSE whose
façade is partially concealed by two SU-
MAC TREES in bloom. A FULL MOON illumi-
nates the trees.

INT. SECOND FLOOR BEDROOM

PRUDENCE, 18, Eurasian, gazes at one
wall covered with her medals, certificates, and awards. Her eyes rest on the
framed PHOTO at the wall's center — a
formal family portrait of Prudence in a
graduation gown; LEO, her father, Chinese, 41, trim, stern; MARGARET, her
mother, Caucasian American, 39, a sub-
limated beauty; her two younger sisters
DENISE, 13, and LORRAINE, 9.

MARK, 20-something, Caucasian American,
waits at the bottom of a LADDER under
her bedroom window.

                    MARK
                (whispers)
          Pru! Prudence!

Prudence, holding a suitcase, leans over
windowsill.

                    PRUDENCE
          (whispers)
     Shh! You'll wake everyone. Catch.

She drops the suitcase out the window.
Mark catches it and falls to the ground.

                    MARK
             (grunts)
          What's in it? Bricks?

Prudence descends the ladder carrying
the family PHOTO under her arm.

                    PRUDENCE
          Close. Books. Botany. Organic chem.
          A surgeon's wife should be well-
          read. An intellectual asset to her
          husband.

Mark embraces her.

                    MARK
          You'd be an intellectual asset with
          or without books. And I'm not a
          surgeon, not…

PRUDENCE

Not yet. But you will be. And I'll
be Mrs. Mark Halpern even sooner.

MARK

Tomorrow. No. Today. In about
(checks his watch) eleven hours.

He picks up suitcase and takes her hand.

PRUDENCE

Haven't you forgotten something?
(laughs softly when he begins to
kiss her) The ladder, silly! It
goes back in garage.

MARK

Pru, this is hardly the time to be
fastidious.

PRUDENCE

It's precisely the time. What will
the neighbors think when they see
a ladder leaning up against my bedroom window?

MARK

What will your parents think — and
what will they DO — when they wake
up because of the racket we're making taking it back to the garage?

> PRUDENCE
>
> It's my parents I'm thinking of. My father especially. The loss of face if the neighbors ever found out that…

> MARK
>
> More than the loss of a daughter? Pru, we've gone over all this before.

> PRUDENCE
>
> Not the ladder part.

> MARK
>
> We can't risk waking them. (looking up at the sumac trees) Besides, you can't even see it through all those branches. They sure could use a trim.

> PRUDENCE
>
> Please, Mark. We'll be extra quiet. Please.

TITLES roll as Prudence and Mark collapse the ladder and take it back to the garage.

                                        FADE TO BLACK

The first thing Margaret did when she opened the door to Prudie's bedroom—not having received an answer to the second, louder set of knocks, indication that something was amiss—was sneeze. Then she saw that the window—the one facing the offending sumac trees—was thrown wide open. She closed it, but not before she noticed the empty but too-carefully made bed and the thin white envelope in the center of it. It was addressed *To My Parents* and it was making her heart race. Margaret stifled a second sneeze and noiselessly closed the bedroom door. She slid a finger under the flap and read the single-page letter inside. She read it a second time, folded it, and placed it back in its envelope which she put deep in her housecoat pocket.

Only then did she notice that Prudie's high school graduation photo was gone. She stared at the empty space it had left for a long moment—as if time could restore what was missing—then began rummaging through the drawers of Prudie's desk. She made a pile of the most important documents: her daughter's high school diploma, valedictory speech, freshman transcript from Barnard College showing all A's and pre-med as her intended major. From the wall, she removed the medals, certificates, and citations, including the second-place medal for the National Spelling Bee Competition and, Margaret's favorite—the first-place trophy for the New York City Catholic Charities Catechism Contest—and added them to the pile.

She stashed the academic bounty in the one suitcase she found in Prudie's closet—the larger of a set of two—which meant that her daughter had left home with its smaller counterpart. The thought of such a dearth of worldly goods brought tears to Margaret's eyes and to her mind the realization that Prudie would soon be a married woman, if she wasn't one already. After the rest of the family was out of the house, she would hide the suitcase in a corner of the attic—a room they used solely for things they no longer had any use for or had completely forgotten.

Margaret put the suitcase back in the closet, patted the letter in her pocket to make sure it was still there, licked her lips that would have to withhold the truth a little longer, and headed downstairs into the lion's den.

Everything had changed. Nothing had changed. Denise and Lorraine sat hunched and half-asleep at the kitchen table, Denise eating her usual bowl of Cheerios with a sliced banana; Lorraine, her everyday concoction of two slices of Wonder Bread toast slathered with butter and drizzled Jackson Pollock-style with Bosco chocolate syrup. Denise was a freshman at the Bronx High School of Science—the only student from St. Agatha's Parochial School's graduating class of 1959 attending a "heathen" high school—a cultural snob and French wannabe. Lorraine was a fourth grader at St. Agatha's Parochial School who loved *The Mickey Mouse Club* and the Irish jig. Still the wife of Leo Lin and the mother of his three daughters, Margaret began brewing a pot of coffee, something she did every day. She set the timer to four and a half minutes and felt the resistance of each turn of the knob.

"Where's Pluto?" Lorraine asked.

"Don't speak with your mouth full. Still sleeping. She was up late. Studying. She has only afternoon classes today. And your sister's name is Prudence, young lady."

"Denise calls her Pluto all the time."

"Rainey's got Pluto on her brain. That's what she gets for watching so much TV." Denise turned to face Lorraine and wheedled, "Miss Mickey Mouse Club."

"Don't let your father catch you watching TV during the week."

Realizing too late that her admonition gave rather than with-
held consent, Margaret pressed her lips together. *Don't watch TV
during the week* was what she should have said. The timer rang. She
pushed down the plunger of the French press and felt the strong
resistance of the coffee grains and the brewed coffee.

Lorraine glanced at her mother to make sure she wasn't looking,
then stuck out her tongue at her sister. "Denise is the mean one."

"I'm just teasing Pluto," Denise retorted. "I'm not ridiculing her."

"What's 'ridiculing'?"

"The way your sister is speaking about Prudence right now."
Margaret shot Denise a warning glance. "Eat your breakfast, both
of you, or you'll be late for school."

When Leo entered the kitchen, he accepted as if by divine right
the mug of coffee Margaret extended to him—black, brewed for
precisely four and a half minutes, half a teaspoon of sugar. This, too,
was part of the daily morning ritual, a small but essential assurance
that all was right in the world. Or that it could be made so, as
long as such rituals were maintained. He was wearing his sum-
mer-weight charcoal gray pin-striped double-breasted suit. This
alerted Margaret to the fact that he would be making a visit to his
close friend and stockbroker, Lao Cao. The suit looked well on him.
As did everything she'd chosen for him. She would have selected
a different tie to go with it, though. Something a bit more colorful.

Leo glanced at his two daughters, the kitchen table littered
with breakfast foods.

"You people are going to eat me out of house and home," he said,
after a sip of coffee. "Where's Prudie?"

"Still asleep," Margaret said. "She was up late studying for some
test or other. I'll wake her in half an hour."

"And your job interview?"

"Not until this afternoon. That's promising, isn't it, that they've called me back for a second one?"

"Punctuality is important. Don't be late. And don't fiddle with your fingers."

Unaware she'd been wringing her hands (for how long?), Margaret stuffed them into her housecoat pockets. The crackle of the letter caused her to wince and hold her breath.

"That's a bad habit you inherited from your mother."

"Shall I pick you up at the station? The usual time?"

Leo nodded and finished his coffee.

"No breakfast?"

"No time," Leo answered from the dining room where he was scrutinizing the contents of his briefcase. "You people," he addressed Denise and Lorraine, "you'd better leave now or you'll be late for school."

Lorraine rose immediately, went to the refrigerator and extracted her lunch box. In defiance of her father, Denise let several seconds elapse before she rose and retrieved her bagged lunch in slow motion.

"Bye, Mom. Bye, Dad," Lorraine chirped before heading out the back door. "Good luck, Mom."

"Bye," Denise said, two steps behind her sister. "Yeah. *Bonne chance.*"

"Thank you, girls. Bye."

The back door slammed shut. Hands still in her pockets, Margaret leaned back against the sink and stared at the kitchen table and its contents, looking at but not seeing them. Briefcase in hand, Leo walked back into the kitchen. Margaret mustered what she hoped would pass for a bright smile, but its wattage must have been very low for her husband to say, assuming she was thinking about her impending interview:

"You really should have more self-confidence."

As if underscoring this character deficiency in his wife, he zipped his briefcase closed and left by way of the front door. Margaret decided to wait a while before burying the treasure chest of Prudie's scholastic accomplishments in a corner of the attic (the one that hosted a hornet's nest). She wanted to make sure that Leo hadn't forgotten anything that required him to retrace his steps and come back into the house. She stood before the large living room window. It afforded a view of front and back walkways both of which converged at the driveway where Lorraine was now dancing the Irish jig (she trips the light fantastic, Margaret thought proudly), followed close behind by Denise, swaying her non-existent hips. Soon the girls would go their separate ways—Lorraine heading to the left to walk to St. Agatha's; Denise cutting across the field of Sutcliffe Country Day School for Boys to descend the long flight of wooden stairs to the City Line bus that would take her to Bronx Science.

Leo wandered into Margaret's field of vision, sauntering down the front yard flagstone path to the driveway, then turning right onto Cranston Road before disappearing from view. It took him fourteen minutes to walk to the subway station to catch the IRT train (he'd timed it) which, in turn, whisked him from the top of the Bronx to the tip of Manhattan. How long it took depended on whether he stayed on the local all the way to Wall Street or changed to the express at 96th Street. Her entire family, all of them taking off in different directions.

Her marriage perhaps most of all. She remembered when she and Leo had first met. A mixer at Columbia University. She'd gotten in with the help of her girlfriend who was a sophomore at Barnard. She remembered what she wore, a beautiful dress à la Christian Dior made by her mother that made her look sophisticated, that made her the belle of the ball. She liked him because he was reserved, refined, dignified, and he was a wonderful dancer. He swept her off her feet. Literally. And the poems, many of which he dedicated to her! His muse, he called her. If his dancing had swept her off her feet, it was his poetry that made her grow wings. She, his polar opposite. The south to his north pole. She, an American working-class girl from Staten Island. He, a Chinese student from a wealthy Shanghainese family. Almost everything in America was strange to him. The culture. The customs. The people. She was eager to introduce him to life in America, and she did so with patience and kindness. He was equally patient and kind with her when, soon after their marriage, they settled in China. There, he introduced her to a life she had only dreamed about. The extravagant dinner and dance parties. The distinguished men. The beautiful women. Their own gracious home that boasted six bedrooms. Six bedrooms! And an amah for every one of their three daughters. But civil war broke out, transforming China into a battleground, transforming the dream into a nightmare, forcing them to return to America where Leo was no longer a pampered Ivy League college student but a businessman with an office on Wall Street, a man with no time for dancing, with no appetite for poetry.

Bert jumped up onto the back of the armchair next to Margaret, poked her arm with his wet nose, interrupting her reverie, as if to remind her that he too was family, and set his shaggy front paws regally on the window still. It was his favorite spot in the entire house and the best place from which to view the outside world.

EXT. BUS STOP

Denise boards the bus and shows her bus
pass to the DRIVER.

DENISE

Bonjour, Monsieur.

He gives her a puzzled look. Denise goes
to back of the bus, sits beside a HAS-
SIDIC man. She inhales deeply.

DENISE

*Ahhh! Quel temps! Il fait beau,
n'est-ce pas, Monsieur?*

He slides away from her. She shrugs and
takes out André Gide's *Le Retour de
l'Enfant Prodigue* from her book bag and
begins reading under her breath.

EXT. SUBWAY STATION

Leo mounts the subway stairs on Wall
Street, begins walking to his office, reconsiders, turns around, heads deter-
minedly in the opposite direction.

INT. LIN HOUSE

Margaret mounts the stairs carrying the
heavy suitcase and puts it in a far corner of the attic. She descends to the
master bedroom, begins to dial a number

on the rotary phone on the night table, reconsiders, places the handset back on the phone cradle.

INT. LAO CAO'S OFFICE

LAO CAO, Leo's good friend and stockbroker is, like Leo, in his early 40s, Chinese, conservative. He wears gold wire-rimmed glasses, brilliantines his hair. His office is neat, orderly and spare, like Lao Cao himself. Leo and Lao Cao converse in Mandarin.

> LAO CAO
> (with calm, kindly formality)

What else could you have done, Lao Lin? Flown to Hong Kong, fired your manager, and replaced him with someone else? That would've solved one problem: a dishonest, disloyal manager...

> LEO
> (puffing angrily on a cigarette)

...who'd already established a rival factory and stolen my best workers — including my foreman — all the while running my factory into the ground.

                    LAO CAO
...and you still would have had to
contend with him as a rival factory owner. You could have done that
— as an absentee landlord living
in the United States. Or you could
have returned to Hong Kong to stake
your claim and continued running
your factory. Relocate. Live there.

Leo crushes his cigarette in the ashtray
on Lao Cao's desk.

                    LEO
How could I relocate my family to
Hong Kong? Their life is here.

INT. MASTER BEDROOM, LIN HOUSE

Margaret changes from her housecoat into
a stylish 1950s Dior-style suit, puts on
artful makeup, and is instantly transformed into a beautiful, sophisticated, self-confident woman. She looks into
the full-length cheval mirror and stands
taller and prouder, moves with grace and
ease, EXUDES elegance and sophistication.
She dons her hat and gloves and picks
up her handbag. She looks like she's
stepped out of the pages of Vogue. She
takes Prudie's LETTER out of her housecoat pocket and puts it in her handbag.
She looks at the telephone, reaches for

the handset, then withdraws her hand and,
with a LORETTA YOUNG-type entrance flourish, she exits the bedroom.

INT. LAO CAO'S OFFICE

Leo gets up from his chair, goes to the
window, lights up another cigarette. Lao
Cao remains seated behind his desk.

> LAO CAO
> Or you could have left your family
> here while you made extended trips
> to Hong Kong to oversee operations.
> That would have been another option.

> LEO
> (shaking his head)
> Me there. Them here. That wouldn't
> have worked. And now with my mother…

He looks out the window to the street
twenty-five stories below.

> LAO CAO
> You see? You did the sensible thing.
> The ONLY sensible thing. You sold
> the factory.

LEO
(self-castigating)

I should have gotten more for it.
I practically GAVE it away.

LAO CAO

Hong Kong real estate these days?
It's a buyer's market. And with Mao
in power, it's only going to get
worse.

LEO

So you think I made the right
choice?

LAO CAO

You could have done nothing — just
walked away — and come away emp-
ty-handed. Instead you sold the
factory, and to the highest bidder.

LEO

To the ONLY bidder. And the bid was
low.

LAO CAO

It was a generous bid, Lao Lin.
Considering it was the only one.
You have to admit, as disloyal as
he was, he had face. And he permit-
ted you to save face.

>   LEO
>   (bitterly)

Adding insult to injury! His bid
was lower than what the factory's
worth. And the fact that it came
from that turtle's egg… (voice cur-
dled in anger) To think he owns my
factory, owns TWO factories.

Leo stubs out his cigarette on the
palm of his hand.

>   LAO CAO
>   (concerned)

Lao Lin, think of it this way: he
MIGHT stay in business. Even make
a profit. But not for long. One, two
years maximum. Electrical condensers are a thing of the past or soon
will be. Electronics. COMPUTERS.
That's where the future lies. COM-
PUTER CHIPS.

>   LEO

Who's to say that bastard isn't
converting to computer chips even
now as we speak — and using MY factory to do it in.

Lao Cao rises from his chair and goes
over to Leo.

                    LAO CAO

Speaking of the future, I met with
Zhang the other day. The immigration lawyer. He brought up my
brother's visa application. And
your mother's.

                    LEO

I'm sorry, Lao Cao. I didn't mean to
be so harsh. You're my oldest friend.
I appreciate your helping me with my
mother's application, as well as with
the sale of the factory.

                    LAO CAO

It's always my pleasure to help you.
We go back a long way. Share a lot
of the same experiences.

LEO nods thoughtfully.

                    LEO

So what did Zhang have to say? How
do your brother's chances look?

                    LAO CAO

Quite good. Actually, very good
(beat) now that I've become an
American citizen. He should be getting his visa in a month.

                    LEO

If you're suggesting that I become
a naturalized American citizen as

well… I'm Chinese. And proud to be.

                    LAO CAO
I'm as proud of my heritage as you
are. But I live in America. I have
for years. I got married here. My
wife was born here. My son was born
here. Our life is in America.

                    LEO
You might live in America, but
don't fool yourself: you'll never
be an American. Not in THEIR eyes.

                    LAO CAO
I bring up the idea of naturalization only because of what Zhang
told me.

                    LEO
And that is?

                    LAO CAO
Your mother's visa application.
It's being held up. It's nothing
personal. It's the political situation between China and the United States. They think that anyone
with ties to the mainland, even
Hong Kong, might be a Communist or
a Communist sympathizer.

                    LEO
So not just my mother but ALL Chinese are suspect. I should feel
grateful that it's not personal.

                   LAO CAO
You can still obtain resident status for her.

                    LEO
How?

                   LAO CAO
Become a naturalized American
citizen.

LEO scoffs.

                   LAO CAO
That's what Zhang suggested. He
said it will work. Guaranteed. It's
your mother's only chance.

                    LEO
Just erase my Chinese heritage of
five thousand years and assimilate
theirs of three hundred. Fill my
daughters' heads will inane television programs and infantile plea-
sures so they forget where they
come from and what their culture
and values are. At least Prudie
hasn't let me down. At least she's
remained Chinese.

Obedient. Cultivated. Studious.
First in her class ever since ele-
mentary school. Two more years and
she'll start medical school. I want
her to be surgeon. A brain surgeon.

                    LAO CAO
All I'm saying is your citizenship
will open the door for your mother. Isn't that what you've been
working towards? For how many years
now? You got her out of China to
Hong Kong. From Hong Kong to Cuba.
She's right on America's doorstep.
There's a rumor going around that
Battista's days are coming to an
end. That a Communist revolution is
afoot. Some fellow named Fidel Cas-
tro. All you have to do is say a
few simple words, sign a few papers.
(seeing a chink in LEO's armor,
says in English) Do it, Leo. She's
your mother. How many years does
she have left? She'll want to spend
them with you.

                              FADE OUT

Denise has a free period which she decides to spend in the school library with her nose buried in *Le retour de l'enfant prodigue*. But as she passes the open doorway of Animal Lab, whose pungent odor announces its whereabouts and precedes it by several feet, a squeaking noise makes her stop and peer inside. A tall (for a Bronx Sciencite), thin student wearing horn-rimmed glasses and a slide rule hooked to his belt loop drops a splayed white mouse into a glass cage containing a garter snake. He taps his slide rule against the rim of the cage.

"Come and get it, swivel hips. Chow time."

Denise recognizes him as a sophomore. They share the same lunch period. He always wears a wool vest in wintertime and plaid shirts in any season. (He's wearing one now.) And thick, ripple-soled lace-up shoes that look like they'll never wear out. (How could they?) He has big feet, and the shoes make them look even bigger. Clodhoppers. He wears his straight brown hair long in front, probably just so it will fall into his eyes and he can send the thick mop back with a flick of his head. He can't use his hands to push it back because he always keeps them both in his pockets. He walks around the school cafeteria with two or three other students (all male), flicking his head, hands shoved into his pockets, clodhoppers on his feet. He doesn't sit at Denise's table. He's an upperclassman, after all. She sits, usually, with two freshman exchange students: the

German Gerhard, who suffers from frequent bloody noses and often has bullet-sized balls of white cotton wool stuffed up each nostril; and Marianne, a Dutch girl, who has a port-wine stain that covers a third of her face. Gerhard and Marianne are not very talkative but when they do speak, their English is heavily accented, which at least sounds more French than American English. Bronx-accented American English, especially.

"*Dégueulasse,*" Denise says loud and clear from the open doorway.

The sophomore turns and mock bows from the waist before he straightens up, flicking back the hair that's fallen over his face.

"At your service. Only it's pronounced Dug-less. Spelled D-O-U-G-L-A-S. Class of '62. And you?"

"*Dégueulasse.* Pronounced Day-gull-ass. Spelled D-E-accent aigu-G-U-E-U-L-A-S-S-E. It means disgusting in French. And that's disgusting what you just did."

"What? Feeding Elvis here. That's my job. Besides, everybody's got a right to eat. Even a snake in the grass—uh, cage, as the case may be."

The snake has caught the mouse. Denise watches, horrified, mesmerized, as the reptile coils tighter and tighter around its prey, squeezing it to death.

"Couldn't you at least feed it a mouse that's already dead," Denise half-accuses, half-begs. "Chloroform the mouse or something?"

"Sorry. No mercy killings allowed. Snakes dig only live meat."

When he picks up another white mouse by its tail and Denise turns to go, he asks:

"Hey, you wouldn't be looking for an extracurricular activity, would you? Tuesdays and Thursdays, 3:15 to 4:15. I could use some help cleaning out the cages. No feedings required."

"Clean out the cages yourself," Denise replies.

To which Douglas responds by hovering the mouse—whiskers

trembling, nose twitching, legs splayed—over the cage of another ravenous snake and letting it fall.

"*Assassin!*" (pronounced à la française) Denise hurls at him before striding off, nose in the air, a sly smile forming on her lips.

Walking home from school, Lorraine broke into the Irish jig. She and her classmates had performed it for the entire school during last month's assembly. She'd practiced for weeks at home. She knew it by heart. She'd danced it perfectly. Sister Patrick even said so, even took her aside right after assembly and told her as much. Well, not in exactly in those words. She had said, exactly, "You dance the Irish jig like it's in your blood and bones, Lorraine. Your mother, lovely woman, she wouldn't be Irish, would she now?"

Lorraine had told her, no, her mother was American. Pressed further by the nun, she'd said her mother's parents came from Czechoslovakia.

"And they're Catholic, am I right? And they raised her as a Catholic?"

When Lorraine had answered yes, she saw Sister Patrick's eyes suddenly change expression, like she was doing arithmetic in her head.

"Lorraine, dear, have you spoken to your father yet? Asked him about what I discussed with you a few days ago? About converting to Catholicism."

Lorraine's blank stare metamorphosed, like she too was doing arithmetic in her head.

"No, Sister Patrick."

That was true. No venial sin there.

"And why haven't you?"

Why hadn't she? Easy. She was afraid of what his answer might be. Was *sure* to be.

"I don't know, Sister Patrick," Lorraine lied.

The if-then continued in her head. Yes, she was afraid of her father. But she was also afraid of Sister Patrick, she of the piercing eyes, the hooked nose, the voluminous black habit. Sister Patrick. The person who gave her tests and marked her report card—test scores and report cards that accurately measured, according to her father, not only Lorraine's intelligence but her very worth. So whom should she be more afraid of disappointing, of disobeying, given that her report card served as the gold standard for her answer?

The nun placed her very clean white hands inside the stiff, even whiter cuffs of her habit. "Such an important matter as the salvation of one's soul shouldn't wait."

"No, Sister Patrick," Lorraine said. "I'll ask him. I'll ask him very soon, when he asks me my catechism questions."

"'Tis a good deed you'll be doing—saving not one but two souls for Christ," the nun assured her. "On Judgment Day, you'll sit that much closer to God's throne in the kingdom of Heaven. You may go now, Lorraine."

"Thank you, Sister Patrick."

Lorraine had fled from the wings of the auditorium stage, almost knocking over a classmate who'd overheard the conversation and who shouted as she shot past:

"Maybe closer to God's throne, but I bet it won't get you on *The Mickey Mouse Club!*"

INT. LIN RESIDENCE — DAY

Lorraine is doing a headstand against
the living room wall and watching Cub-
by and Karen tap dancing on The Mickey
Mouse Club. Her feet mimic their dance
steps. Denise strides angrily into the
room and takes the leash off Bert, who
assumes his usual position on the back
of the armchair. Denise turns off the TV.

                    LORRAINE
          Hey! Turn that back on.

                    DENISE
          Daddy'll kill you if he catches you
          watching that garbage.

                    LORRAINE
                (righting herself)
          You're not Daddy.

                    DENISE
          Thank God.

Lorraine turns the TV back on.

                    LORRAINE
          It's not nice to take the name of
          the Lord Thy God in vain.

Denise plunks herself down on the sofa.

                    DENISE
Pluto still not home? It was her
turn to walk Bert, not mine.

                    LORRAINE
          (resuming her headstand against
          the wall)
Look who's talking. Prudie walks
Bert when you're late from school.
And you're late a lot.

                    DENISE
          (haughtily)
It just so happens I'm involved in
a number of extra-curricular activities. French language lab. French
club. Extracurricular activities
are important for getting into college. Especially for people like
us. They want well-rounded students,
not one-sided bookworms.

                    LORRAINE
They took Prudie, didn't they? And
she's a bookworm.

                    DENISE
That's different. According to Daddy,
she's a genius. (in LEO's voice)
"Graduated from Hunter College High
School at 15. Accepted to Barnard
College on a full scholarship."

KATRINKA, the Lin BUICK, pulls up in the driveway. Bert barks and heads for the back door.

> DENISE
>
> Speak of the dev… uh, Daddy.

Lorraine rights herself and turns off the TV. She and Denise head for the back door. Leo, who looks irritated, enters followed by Margaret, who looks elated.

> DENISE
>
> Don't tell me. You got the job.

> MARGARET
>
> I start tomorrow.

> DENISE
> (in French)
>
> Formidable!

Lorraine squeals with delight and hugs her mother.

> LEO
>
> It's about time someone around here started helping me pay the bills. The way you people spend money, you'd think it grows on trees. (to DENISE and LORRAINE) Set the table. It's almost dinnertime. (to MARGA-RET) Tell Prudie to come down and help her sisters.

Leo heads up the stairs. Margaret follows after him, her formerly beaming
face now ashen and drawn. Denise and
Lorraine clear the dining room table
of their school books and begin to set
the table. LOUD, CRASHING NOISES. They
freeze, stare at each other with fear
in their eyes, then race up the stairs,
Bert bounding behind them.

They enter Prudie's room to find Leo in
a frenzy, tearing what plaques and certificates Margaret didn't salvage from
the wall and bookshelves and throwing
them onto the floor, followed by the contents of her dresser drawers and closets.
Prudie's LETTER lies in pieces on her
bed. Margaret, in a corner of the room,
is the picture of strained forbearance.

                    LEO
          (searching through the pile on
          the floor)

Where are they? Her high school diploma. The rest of her medals and
awards. WHERE ARE THEY?

                    MARGARET
          (in a small voice)

She must have taken them with her.

LEO
(to DENISE and LORRAINE)

Go get me some empty rice sacks
from the basement.

Lorraine looks at Leo as if she doesn't
understand what he's saying, Denise as
if he's a madman.

LEO

What are you waiting for? Do as
I say!

Denise and Lorraine leave after a moment's hesitation.

MARGARET

Leo...

LEO

Don't you dare talk back to me! Why
didn't you tell me what was going
on behind my back?

MARGARET

I had no idea that...

LEO

What kind of mother are you that
you didn't know what your daughter
was up to? Go down to the basement
and tell your daughters to bring
all the rice sacks here, then start
filling them with Prudie's things.

I don't want a single trace of her
left in this house.

                                        CUT

For someone like Denise, a tween who didn't possess a green thumb and who lived most of the time in an imaginary world of her own design, the Lin house was a ball and chain around her ankle, especially on weekends. The half-timbered Dutch Tudor located on a private road in a sylvan New York suburban neighborhood was the medieval dungeon in which life had thrown her, complete with instruments of torture and no means of escape. Instead of the dank, dark rooms and the surrounding moat across which there was no drawbridge, there were four large lawns to mow every Saturday—spring, summer, and fall. The Back Yard Big Hill (Prudie's job). The adjacent Back Yard Little Hill (also, Prudie's). The House Front Yard, which actually consisted of two lawns separated by a flagstone path (Denise's job). The House Side Yard (also Denise's job). And the Street Front Yard (Lorraine's job), so called to distinguish it from the House Front Yard and because it was situated on the same level as Cranston Road, whereas the House Front Yard, together with house and property, was five feet higher, set up on an embankment held in place by a fieldstone wall.

Not only were there lawns to mow, there were English ivy and azalea and hydrangea bushes to trim; flowerbeds to plant, weed and water; and the autumnal sheddings of oak, dogwood, and sumac to rake up, put into sacks and, when sufficiently dry, set ablaze in the fire pit in a corner of the Back Yard Little Hill.

Only today, it wasn't unwanted vegetation that needed to be consumed by fire but a human sacrifice—Prudence Lin, via her possessions—to appease the gods of wrath and reciprocity. Overseeing the propitiatory ritual was its self-appointed high priest, father of the reprobate/offering/victim. It was a macabre sight. Leo's face contorted with rage, grief and an eerie kind of fascination, even ecstasy, as he stood looking into the flames. The sinking sun making long shadows of Denise and Lorraine as they carried burlap sacks of their absconded sister's belongings on their backs from house to fire pit for their father to throw into the bonfire. And Margaret, mater dolorosa, thumbless vestal virgin, motionless silent witness.

Lorraine set down the sack she was carrying.

"I'm tired, and hungry. When can we eat?"

"Soon," her mother assured her. "Very soon. We're almost finished."

One by one, Leo threw the contents of the sack Lorraine had handed him onto the fire, which roared higher with each offering. Denise watched them smolder, catch fire, and burn.

"Well, at least I won't have to wear Prudie's hand-me-downs anymore."

Margaret looked on with no palpable change of expression. She had made those clothes. Prudie's high school graduation dress of Italian silk with Belgian lace at the collar and cuffs. Up in flames. The Chanel-like suit of bouclé wool with thick woven braid trim. Up in flames. The pleated skirt. Up in flames. The A-line skirt. Up in flames. The full skirt. Up in flames. The boxy, waist-length forest-green wool jacket with welt seams and bound buttonholes. Up in flames. The gabardine scarlet-red princess-line spring coat with brushed gold buttons. Up in flames. The Prussian-blue car coat. All of them up in smoke and flame.

"Can I move into Prudie's room, now that she's eloped?"

LESLIE LI

45

When her mother blocked out her daughter's question by closing her eyes and tightening her mouth, Denise avoided her displeasure by moving closer to Leo and the fire. *"Quel chaleur!"*

"Leo, Denise, you're both too close to the fire."

As if to prove his wife wrong, Leo grabbed the sack out of Denise's arms and, in one fell swoop, emptied all the clothes in it onto the conflagration. Flames, sparks, and embers shot out in all directions. Burning jackets, charred dresses, smoldering skirts extruded out from under the new load of clothing like molten lava from an erupting volcano. Denise felt as if a solid wall of unbearable heat had slammed into her. She shut her eyes, covered her face with her forearm and backed away. When she lowered her arm, her father's pant leg was on fire.

"Daddy!"

She lurched towards him, grabbed the empty rice sack out of his hands, and smothered the flames flickering on the cuff of his left pant leg.

Margaret pulled both Leo and Denise away from the bonfire.

"Leo, are you all right? Let me see your leg." She pulled up his pant leg, then shut her eyes in relief. A small area. Only first degree. "Denise," she said. "Your hands."

"No, nothing. The burlap. I'm fine."

Lorraine clutched at her mother. "Mommy, I'm scared."

Margaret cradled her daughter's head with one hand and patted her back with the other. Baffled, Denise stared at her father's face. No expression. No indication of pain. Nothing. He didn't *feel* it, she thought. He didn't feel a thing.

"Let me put something on that burn," Margaret said, turning towards the house.

Leo remained rooted in place. "We finish this first."

"You don't want it to get infected, otherwise...."

"I said we finish what we started. I don't want a single thing left to remind me of…that traitor. You will never mention her name again, do you understand? None of you. Again. Ever."

He looked unseeing into the bonfire.

"She's dead."

That evening, the Lins ate in almost total silence. They'd never been much for conversation at the dinner table. Meals were for eating, after all, not for talking. Talking disturbed good digestion and the pleasure of eating good food. But tonight, the silence was oppressive and the few words spoken startled, like the sound of a rock dropped inside a well one thought was filled with water but that was dry as dust. Like the sound of a bird crashing into a window it had thought was air. Like the sound of thunder following a bolt of lightning—thunder that was an earth-shuddering, animal-like groan instead of the anticipated short, swift crack, like the snapping of a desiccated branch.

"Can I have the platter of fried chicken?" Thump.

"Pass the bowl of mashed potatoes, please." Thud.

"Lorraine, how about a serving of string beans? I don't see anything green on your plate." Rumble.

Then silence would swallow them up again, lifting their shoulders closer to their ears, making their movements stiffer, their mastication longer, more laborious. The dearth of speech, the space devoid of sound, was most palpable around Prudence's chair, her conspicuous absence. As though obeying the physical law that states that Nature abhors a vacuum, Bert jumped up and filled her vacant seat and began begging for food.

"Bert, get down from there!"

Leo tipped the chair and Bert slid off, taking refuge beside Lorraine.

"Bad dog. Bad Bert," she scolded, bending down and shaking her fork on whose tines two limp string beans were impaled.

Her parents weren't looking, so she shook harder.

"Bad, bad Bert," she castigated. Off came the beans first onto the dining room floor, then into Bert's mouth. "Good boy," she whispered, scratching him behind his soft floppy ears. "Eat your veggies."

Her bedroom window = the television screen.
The venetian blinds = the Magic Window.
The *ailanthus altissima* = the Magic Crayons.
Winky Dink and You = her alternative universe.

That night Denise lies in bed staring at the shadows cast on the venetian blinds by the fluttering leaves of the sumac tree outside her window. Because of the full moon, the contrast between light and dark, between amorphous and defined—the tint of nothing and the shade of something—is more sharply delineated on the closed blinds than if there were no moon or a partial one and just the street lamp to serve as backlighting. Her parents are downstairs seated before the television set pretending to watch the news whose litany of horrors are a welcome relief to but a superficial distraction from what—whom—their minds are involuntarily but helplessly focused on. Unable to fall asleep (which Lorraine has succeeded in doing), Denise gets up, opens the door to Prudie's room, steps inside, and carefully closes the door behind her. Even in the dark, she sees that the room is empty. The walls. The shelves. The clothes closet. The chest of drawers. Even the drawers of Prudie's desk and vanity table.

She goes to the window facing Cranston Road, which is almost completely obscured by the branches of the pollen-shedding stinkweed tree as Denise's mother calls the sumac, the tree which almost completely conceals the window from which Prudie made her nocturnal escape. Denise unlocks and pushes both window-panes open all the way. She catches sight of the moon, round as round can be, cradled between two branches.

"Il pleure dans mon coeur comme il pleut sur la ville. Quelle est cette langueur qui pénètre mon coeur?" (My heart weeps tears like rain falling on the city. What is this melancholy that lances my heart?) It's a quote from a poem by Paul Verlaine. It comes to her unbidden. She knows it by heart but this is the first time she actually *feels* it. She leans out the window and touches the leaves that are closest, small hands that extend themselves to hers to be stroked, to be grasped. She looks up at the moon again. *"Quelle est cette langueur qui pénètre mon coeur?"* (What is this melancholy that lances my heart?)

She shuts the window, exits the room, closes the door behind her, enters the bedroom she shares with Lorraine, gets back into bed, pulls the covers up to her chin, looks at the venetian blind, Winky Dink's Magic Window. The Magic Crayons/sumac leaves have created something strange, something unexpected. Something *significant.* She knows it's significant because her breath catches in her throat and her entire body tenses slightly. Transfixed, she stares at the huge bed that appears on the venetian blind, filling it almost to its edges. From the lower right-hand corner, a small child of indeterminate sex appears, maybe two, three years old. Like the TV cartoons Denise favored in her youth—Betty Boop, Popeye, Krazy Kat—everything is in black and white. But like Walt Disney's movie *Fantasia,* the images are less stylized, more realistic, almost three dimensional, and not confined to the two dimensional Magic Window but rising out of it, here in bas-relief, there in haut-relief. The child especially is prominent. It toddles to the bed, kneels, and begins to crawl under it. And there it stays, half in and half out. Head and torso concealed, raised buttocks, legs and feet exposed. Is the child looking for something? Is it hiding from something? Someone? Doesn't the child know that anybody can see it but it can't see them, that it's visible to everyone except itself?

EXT. LIN RESIDENCE - SATURDAY

We see the Lin family at their weekend
outdoor chores. Leo is cutting back the
English ivy at the foot of the Back Yard
Big Hill. Visible is the fire pit of the
Back Yard Little Hill and the charred
remains of Prudie's possessions. Margaret is tending her flower garden that
borders the House Front Lawn where Lorraine is pulling up crab grass. Denise
is mowing the Back Yard Big Hill. She
slips and falls.

                    DENISE
          Zut, alors! Merde!

INT. LIN RESIDENCE - LATER THAT DAY

We see the Lin family at their weekend
indoor chores. Margaret is waxing the
kitchen floor, tap dancing with the mop as
she goes. She's good. When Leo passes by,
she stops, embarrassed. Lorraine is vacu-
uming the upstairs hall carpet. Denise is
washing the upstairs hall bathroom.

                    DENISE
          Merde! Merde! Merde! Merde and pox
          on you, Prudie! You get freedom and
          what do I get? YOUR back lawns to
          mow. YOUR bathroom to clean. YOUR
          time slot for walking Bert. In ad-
          dition to all my own chores.

                         LORRAINE
                (turning off the vacuum cleaner)

Hey, what about me? What about Mom?
We got saddled with Prudie's chores,
too, you know. At least we don't
have tospend Saturdays at Grampa's anymore learning Chinese from
Aiying.

                         DENISE

And what about Daddy? We're just a
bunch of slaves doing his bidding.
That's why Prudie eloped. Somebody
should tell him slavery was abol-
ished in the United States almost a
century ago.

                         LORRAINE
                      (puzzled)

I thought it was because she fell
in love.

                         DENISE

I bet he's in his room right now,
feet up on his desk, laughing at us.

We see Leo at his desk in the MASTER
BEDROOM smoking a cigarette, poring over
the US NATURALIZATION MANUAL and filling
out the application for citizenship.

                    LEO
          (murmuring as he reads and
          writes; we alternate between
          seeing Leo and the application
          he's filling in)
     Name (writes) Lin Li Hou. (eras-
     es, writes instead) Leo Lin. Age
     (writes) 41. Place of birth (writes)
     Shanghai, Jiangsu Province, China.
     No. (erases, writes) The People's
     Republic of China. Higher Education
     (writes) Fudan University, Shanghai,
     two years. Graduated Columbia Uni-
     versity with degrees in political
     science and international relations.
     Marital Status (writes) Married.
     Number of children (writes) Three.
     (erases, writes) Two.

     He stands, balls up the application, and
     throws it into the wastepaper basket
     next to his desk. He picks up the manual
     and turns to the PLEDGE OF ALLEGIANCE.

                    LEO
          (reading the instructions)
     Right hand over heart. (does this,
     then reads in a monotone) I pledge
     allegiance to the flag of the United
     States of America. And to the re-
     public for which it stands. One na-
     tion. Under God. Indivisible. With
     liberty and justice for all.

Leo slaps the manual down on his desk,
opens a desk drawer, takes out the magazine CHINA RECONSTRUCTS. The telephone
on his nightstand rings. He looks at it
but doesn't pick up.

In the KITCHEN, Margaret picks up the
handset of the extension on the wall.

                    MARGARET
          Hello. Lin residence.

                    MISS ST-PETER
          Miss Lin, this is Miss St-Peter,
          the hat buyer at Saks Fifth Avenue.
          I hope I'm not disturbing you — on
          the weekend and all.

                    MARGARET
                    (apprehensive, leaning against
                    the mop)
          Not at all. How are you, Miss
          St-Peter?

                    MISS ST-PETER (O.S.)
          Fine. Fine, thank you, Miss Lin.

                    MARGARET
          Is something the matter?

                    MISS ST-PETER
          Do you remember a woman of a cer-
          tain age who bought three Lilly
          Daché hats from you yesterday?

MARGARET

Mrs. Arthur Fanning. I remember her
well. Not only did she buy three
hats, she knew exactly which ones
suited her best.

MISS ST-PETER

Mrs. Fanning is Mr. Bernstein's
mother-in-law.

MARGARET
(blanches)

Mr. Bernstein, the president of the
store?

MISS ST-PETER

Mrs. Fanning told Mr. Bernstein
that you spent your lunch hour
helping her choose not only the
hats but also the accessories that
would complement them. Gloves.
Scarves. Jewelry.

MARGARET

Miss St-Peter, I apologize if I've
broken any of the store's regu-
lations. I wasn't aware that as a
saleswoman I'm not allowed to con-
sort with…

<pre>
                    MISS ST-PETER
Mr. Bernstein is very fond of his
mother-in-law. More than that, he
LISTENS to her. Mrs. Fanning told
him that you're being wasted as a
saleswoman in the millinery depart-
ment — that you have EXTRAORDINARY
fashion sense — her own words — the
kind of fashion sense that Saks
Fifth Avenue is known for all over
the world. I hate to be losing you,
Miss Lin. In the short amount of
time that you've been in my depart-
ment, you've been nothing but an
asset, but I…

                    MARGARET
                 (crestfallen)
You're firing me.

                    MISS ST-PETER
You're being promoted.

                    MARGARET
                  (stunned)
Promoted?

                    MISS ST-PETER
To where your talents can be put to
best use. In the fashion depart-
ment. Window displays, primarily.
In charge of accessories. The pro-
motion comes with a commensurate
</pre>

increase in salary, of course. One
hundred dollars more biweekly than
you're earning now. Miss Lin. Are
you still there?

MARGARET

I don't know what to say.

MISS ST-PETER

Say yes! Say you'll take the
position!

MARGARET

Yes. Yes, I will. I most certainly will. Thank you, Miss St-Peter.
Thank you very much.

MISS ST-PETER

Oh, not my doing. I'm just the
bearer of glad tidings. Just report
to the fashion department on the
sixth floor nine o'clock on Monday.
And you'll be taking a two-hour
lunch that day. Mr. Bernstein's or-
ders. For the hour you spent with
his mother-in-law. Have a good
weekend, Miss Lin.

MARGARET

The same to you, Miss St-Peter.

Margaret hangs up the phone and attacks
the kitchen floor with gusto. Her tap
dancing is freer, breezier, and she uses

the mop as a romantic partner, Fred Astaire to her Ginger Rogers. Denise and
Lorraine peek in on her from the doorway.

>   LEO (O.S., YELLS)
> Lorraine!

>   DENISE
> Ha! You're in for it.

>   LORRAINE
>   (yells from the bottom of the
>   stairs)
> Yes?

>   LEO (O.S.)
> Come upstairs. I'll ask you your
> catechism questions.

In the MASTER BEDROOM, Leo closes the
naturalization manual in his hand and
shuts his eyes.

>   LEO
>   (reciting under his breath)
> I pledge allegiance. To the flag.
> Of the United States of America.
> And to the republic. For which it
> stands. One nation. Under God. In-
> divisible. With liberty. And jus-
> tice. (smirks) For all.

In her BEDROOM, Lorraine opens her catechism to the chapter "Confirmation," flips

back to the chapter "Baptism," which she
reads quickly under her breath.

> LORRAINE
>
> "What is Baptism? Baptism is the
> sacrament that gives our souls the
> new life of sanctifying grace by
> which we become children of God and
> heirs of heaven." (shuts her eyes)
> Baptism is the sacrament that gives
> our souls…

> LEO (O.S.)
>
> Lorraine!

> LORRAINE
> (hurrying out of her bedroom,
> yells)
>
> Coming, Daddy! (reads from the cat-
> echism in her hands) "What sins
> does Baptism take away? Baptism
> takes away original sin; and also
> actual sins and all the punish-
> ment due to them, if the person be
> guilty of any actual sins and truly
> sorry for them."

Lorraine takes a deep breath, knocks,
then opens the master bedroom door.

In the KITCHEN, Margaret looks at Bert,
who is whimpering outside the doorway.
He starts to enter.

                    MARGARET

Oh, no, you don't. Not on my new-
ly waxed floor. (to DENISE) Take him
out. Poor thing. He needs to go.

                    DENISE

It's not my turn.

                    MARGARET
            (holds out BERT'S leash)

It is now.

In the MASTER BEDROOM, Leo swivels
around in his desk chair to face Lorraine who stands before him.

                     LEO
            (reading from the catechism)

"What are the effects of the character imprinted on the soul by
Baptism?"

                    LORRAINE
            (her hands clasped behind her
            back)

The effects of the character imprinted on the soul by Baptism
are that we become members of the
Church, subject to its laws and
(louder) capable of receiving the
other sacraments. (beat) Like
Matrimony.

                    LEO
              (puzzled)

Where do you see that? Wait a minute. Didn't I ask you these questions last week?

                  LORRAINE
              (C.U. of her crossing her index
              and middle fingers of her right
              hand)

Sister Patrick wants us to review
the chapter on Baptism. (C.U. of
her crossing those same fingers of
her left hand) We're having a test
on it. On Monday.

                    LEO
              (reads from catechism, disin-
              terested)

"Why is Baptism necessary for the
salvation of all men?"

                  LORRAINE

Baptism is necessary for the salvation of all men because Christ said,
"Unless a man be born again of water
and the Spirit, he cannot enter the
kingdom of God."

                    LEO
              (reads, almost terminally
              bored)

"How can those be saved who through
no fault of their own have not received the sacrament of Baptism?"

                    LORRAINE
Like you, Daddy.

Leo flinches and looks up at Lorraine.

                    LORRAINE
It's not your fault that you ha-
ven't been baptized. That's what
Sister Patrick said.

                       LEO
              (sitting up straighter in his
              chair)
Is that what she said? What else
did Sister Patrick say?

                    LORRAINE
That you're a heathen. But only because you were born in China. But
now that you're in America, you can
be saved.

                       LEO
              (leaning forward slightly)
Really?

> LORRAINE
> (showing off her knowledge)

See? (points to a paragraph on the catechism page) It says so, right there. You can be saved through baptism of blood or baptism of desire.

> LEO
> (reads)

"Baptism of blood. When he suffers martyrdom for the faith of Christ."

> LORRAINE

Like the Christians who were thrown to the lions in the Coliseum.

> LEO
> (reads)

"Baptism of desire. When he loves God above all things and desires to do all that is necessary for salvation."

> LORRAINE

No contest. If I were you, I'd choose baptism of desire. Then you can marry Mommy.

> LEO

Your mother and I are already married.

                    LORRAINE

At the last parent-teacher con-
ference, Mommy told Sister Patrick
that you were married outside the
Church. Sister Patrick thinks you
and Mommy should get married INSIDE
the Church.

                    LEO
            (stifling his growing anger)

What for?

                    LORRAINE

For your immortal souls. She says,
that is, Sister Patrick says, that
if you don't get married inside the
Church then both your souls — yours
and Mommy's — will burn in ever-
lasting hellfire.

                    LEO
            (repressing his rage)

You tell your Sister Patrick, you
tell that nun, that I'm a Buddhist.
A Buddhist. You tell her that.

EXT. CRANSTON ROAD

Denise is walking Bert when she sees
Douglas and a FRIEND tossing a football
back and forth. They start coming towards her.

                         DENISE
         Zut! Of all people! Come on, Bert.
         (tugs his leash) Come on, I said!

         Bert stops, holds his ground, and def-
         ecates just as Douglas and his Friend
         arrive.

                         DOUGLAS
         Cute pooch. Short legs for a cocker
         spaniel, though.

                         FRIEND
         What's his name?

                         DENISE
         Bert. Short for Bertram. (super-
         cilious) He's a pedigreed cocker
         spaniel, for your information. His
         mother and father were both champi-
         on show dogs. Bozo Red and Leonard
         Belle.

                         DOUGLAS
         Yeah. I can see the Bozo in him,
         all right. Look at those outsized
         paws. Clown feet. (bends down and
         inspects Bert's turd) Can I make a
         suggestion? Cut back on the veggies.
         His stool will be firmer.

                    FRIEND

Hey, what are you, Doug? A
veterinarian?

                    DOUGLAS

Not a bad profession. Vets earn
more than physicians.

                    FRIEND
                (walking ahead)

C'mon. We're gonna be late.

                    DOUGLAS
                (to DENISE)

Got the time?

                    DENISE

Ten to.   ·

                    DOUGLAS

Ten to what?

                    DENISE

Tend to your own business.

Douglas's Friend throws his arms up
overhead, signifying touchdown.

                    FRIEND

Whoooo-hoo! Goal! Straight through
the uprights! She had you out of
position, Doug.

Douglas's Friend cocks his arms and

sends the football towards him. The
ball sails over Douglas's head and lands
smack in Bert's fresh turd. Horrified,
Denise wipes the ball on the ground and
sheepishly offers it to Douglas who, giv-
en the opportunity that Bert is peeing,
holds it under the stream of urine.

                    DOUGLAS
        Simple hygiene. Urine acts as an
        antiseptic. See how much you could
        learn from me in the animal lab?

                    FRIEND
        C'mon, Doug. Let's get a move on.

Douglas and his Friend walk away. M.S.
of their backs.

                    FRIEND
        Who was that, anyway?

                    DOUGLAS
        Nobody. Some girl at school.

                                        FADE OUT

"I hate this hat. In fact, I hate this dress," Denise said, pulling at the two puckered areas of the bodice that her older sister's breasts had filled. "Another one of Prudie's hand-me-downs that doesn't fit."

Margaret rearranged the leghorn straw hat on her daughter's head and straightened the grosgrain ribbon bow. There was nothing she could do, however, about the deflated bodice. Luckily, the dress had escaped the bonfire since it already hung in Denise's closet.

"It looks fine. Prudie just filled it out a little more, that's all. Where are your white gloves?" she asked Lorraine, who extended her hands to her mother. "Are they clean?

"This crinoline is so itchy."

"But look at how full it makes your skirt. Like a ballerina's tutu."

That did the trick. There were times when suffering for beauty trumped the pleasure of comfort, and any reference to the art of dance numbed Lorraine's perceived pain.

Margaret checked her youngest daughter's anklets and nodded: they were the same color. Of the same pair. The second blare from Katrinka's horn—longer than the first—indicated that Leo was becoming impatient. Before shooing her daughters out the front door, she took a quick look at her own image in the hallway mirror. Chanel-type navy-and-cream pebble-tweed sheath and matching jacket with three-quarter-length sleeves and navy grosgrain trim. Three-quarter-length cream-colored kidskin gloves. Navy calfskin

LESLIE LI   69

handbag. Navy straw boater set firmly on her head atop her smooth cap of hair with its side-swept bangs, its *guiches* tucked behind her ears. She'd seen the hairstyle on Michelle Morgan. One of her customers had remarked that Margaret resembled the elegant French actress. It was probably the coiffure that elicited the comparison, nothing more. Still, whenever she caught her reflection in a mirror, she searched for any similarity other than that hairstyle.

Leo's third and longest blast from Katrinka pulled Margaret from her reverie and out the door. She slid into the passenger side of the idling Buick, cast an apologetic glance at Leo, closed the door, and glanced at her watch. Twenty minutes before Mass began. She always looked forward to Mass on Sunday. The ritual of it. The spectacle of it. The *theatricality* of it. Mass thrilled and saddened her at one and the same time.

"You'll come back for us in an hour?"

It was the question she asked Leo every Sunday when he dropped his family off at church. Invariably, she received his routine response—a distracted nod suggesting that his thoughts had already wandered to more important matters, like the Sunday papers and what news they might contain.

Margaret and her two daughters entered the nave, chose a pew in the center, and took their seats. She looked around surreptitiously, turning her head as minimally as possible and circling her eyes as much as she could, drinking in her surroundings while feigning complete indifference to them. The tabernacle on the altar. The marble statuary. The frescoes on the walls. The congregation all around her. She felt like a guest in the house of God. A guest with all the privileges that implied, and not a family member with all the obligations that exacted.

After Leo dropped his family at church, he drove a few blocks to

Freddie's Corner Soda Fountain and Luncheonette. While he was choosing *The Sunday Times* and *The Daily News* from the newspaper rack, the radio was broadcasting a news program about Red China, communism, and the dangers that country and its political system posed to Western democracy. The new soda jerk behind the counter tilted his chin, and the two coffee-drinking, elbow-leaning customers seated in front of him swiveled around on their stools. Putting two and two together—what they were hearing over the airwaves and the Oriental man rummaging through the newspaper rack—they felt they had the right to take the offensive.

"Darn shame what's happening in China, wouldn't you say?" the soda jerk muttered, loud enough for Leo to hear.

"What China? To the *neighborhood*," one of the customers replied.

A snigger from the speaker. A guffaw from his companion. A snort from the soda jerk. Simultaneously.

Leo ignored them and paid the cashier. As he always did every Sunday morning after driving his family to church and picking up the papers at the luncheonette, he walked to Moskowitz's Bakery three stores up the block. When he pushed open the glass door, part of the *Sunday Times* slid out from under his arm onto the floor.

"The world situation can't be as bad as all that," Mrs. Moskowitz said from behind the counter.

Mr. Moscowitz retrieved the *Business* section and returned it to Leo.

"Thank you."

"Good morning, Mr. Lin. It's always a good morning when I see my best customer. Actually in your corner of the world, it's nothing but good news—nothing short of a miracle. Thirty pound cabbages. Wheat fields so dense school children can dance on top of them. *Mazel tov!* There's no telling what hard work and a resilient spirit can do." He held up his paper coffee cup and boomed, "Here's to

Mao Tse-tung!"

"Not so loud, Marty," Mrs. Moscowitz hissed.

"What, Esther? There's no one here but us chickens…"

Mr. Moscowitz chuckled, which diverted Leo's thoughts to that Western folktale, the line about St. Nick's belly shaking like a bowl full of jelly.

"…unless, of course, Joe McCarthy's hiding under the rugelach."

"Speaking of rugelach," Mrs. Moskowitz interceded, "I just baked a bunch of cinnamon raisin. Fresh out of the oven, Mr. Lin. The apricot, they came out ten minutes ago, no more than that."

"How many dozen can I get for you, Mr. Lin?" Mr. Moskowitz said, joining his wife behind the counter.

"Your husband is a very good businessman," Leo acknowledged.

"Not as good a businessman as my wife is a baker. She's what makes this shop tick."

"Stop it, Marty. You want maybe to see me blush in front of Mr. Lin?"

"One prune hamantaschen for my wife. One apricot for me. Two chocolate horns for the girls. And…

"You mean *three*, don't you, Mr. Lin?" Mrs. Moscowitz said, her hand hovering over the tray of chocolate horns.

"Of course. I meant three."

"And a baker's dozen and a half on the rugelach," Mr. Moscowitz concluded, filling the box his wife handed him. "Ten cinnamon raisin and nine apricot. I should know that by now. Every first Sunday of the month, it's dinner at your father's house. And rugelach is his favorite dessert. The man's got good taste!"

"Oh, Marty. Shush!"

"You're a very lucky man, Mr. Lin, to have your loved ones so close by."

Her husband's declaration brought tears to his wife's eyes. She was able to box and tie Leo's purchases and hand them to him before she reached for a Kleenex to dab at her eyes and blow her nose.

"Allergies," she said. "It's the season."

"I'm sorry to hear it. My wife suffers from the same thing. The pollen."

After Leo paid and wished the couple a good day and till next Sunday, he heard Mrs. Moskowitz say just as the heavy glass door slowly closed behind him, "Such a close-knit family. There's no greater blessing."

Tall, stooped white-haired Monsignor Riordan faced the altar and with both hands raised the Sacred Host over his head. The entire congregation—hands clasped and knees bent in prayer—bowed their heads. All except Denise, who looked at Lorraine as the catechism whizz kid murmured under her breath: "He took bread, blessed and broke it, and giving it to His apostles, said: 'Take and eat'…"

"This is my Body," Monsignor Riordan enunciated in Latin before he placed the Host in his mouth, bowed his head and clasped his hands together. Then he raised the Chalice containing God's Blood and, like the Host, raised it over his head with both hands.

"Then he took a cup of wine, blessed it," Lorraine murmured, head bowed, eyes closed, "and giving it to them, said, 'All of you drink of this; for'…"

"This is my Blood," Monsignor Riordan announced in Latin.

"… 'of the new covenant,'" Lorraine continued, "'which is being shed for many unto the forgiveness of sins.'"

Margaret furtively poked Lorraine in the ribs with her elbow. This gave Denise license to whisper in her sister's ear, "This is Mass. Not a catechism quiz."

Monsignor Riordan lowered the Chalice to his mouth and

took a sip of wine that his proclamation as Christ-on-earth had turned into Blood. He wiped the rim of the Chalice his lips had touched with a clean white handkerchief and set the receptacle back on the altar. Then, flanked by two altar boys, he descended the two steps leading to the altar rail where communicants—Denise and Lorraine among them—were already heading to receive Holy Communion.

For Denise, Holy Communion came with its own set of trials and prerequisites. Transformed into the Body of Christ, the Host would inevitably stick to the roof of her mouth and she would have to pry off it with her tongue—no sacrilegious fingers or teeth allowed. There was no receiving Holy Communion if you hadn't gone to Confession and told your sins ("ratted on yourself," was the way Denise saw it) to the priest, who would expunge them with an appropriate Penance: a series of Hail Marys and/or Our Fathers depending on whether your sins were venial or mortal and how many times you committed each one. Though your Confession was a private affair between confessee and confessor and took place in the sound-proof confessional box, your Penance was on public display for all to see—all those in church awaiting their turn to be, like you, absolved of their sins, all those who could tell by the amount of time you spent kneeling before the altar doing your Penance whether your moral misdeeds were large or small, few or many. And so it was the same with Holy Communion. Everyone at Mass could see whether or not you walked to the altar rail or remained seated in your pew. They could therefore make the following deduction: those receiving Holy Communion had gone to Confession, were absolved of their sins, had said their penance, and now possessed souls white enough to receive Holy Communion; those not receiving Holy Communion hadn't gone to Confession, were saddled with their sins that blackened their souls which made them impure and thus unfit to receive Holy Communion. Everyone in church could see—and judge—who was a devout Catholic this week and who was not.

Margaret remained immobile in her pew, waiting for the feelings of longing and ostracism to subside. Raised Catholic, she had attended Mass on Sunday, gone to Confession, said Penance, received Holy Communion. But in marrying Leo, in marrying outside the Church and its sacrament of Matrimony, she had forfeited the right to receive Communion, together with the prerequisite rituals of Confession and Penance. Every time she attended Sunday Mass, she felt like a tolerated guest, one granted certain privileges but also denied the rights and the responsibilities that a family member—no matter how distant—was privy to.

To diminish both the yearning to belong and the pain of being excluded, she directed her attention to the priest's thickly brocaded chasuble. To the carved marble statues of the Virgin Mary with Child, of St. Joseph. To the cherubim and seraphim painted on the church ceiling. To the gorgeous flower arrangements exuding their heady—even aphrodisiacal—scent more potent than incense. And she envisioned Prudie in the beautiful wedding gown she would have made for her walking gracefully down the center aisle of St. Agatha's Church—a figment of her imagination that dissipated as the solid forms of Denise and Lorraine bore down on her, tongues working to dislodge the Host from the roof of their mouths.

INT. LIN RESIDENCE - SUNDAY, EARLY AFTERNOON

The Lins are in the living room, each
reading a different section of the SUNDAY
PAPERS. Leo is ensconced in his favorite
armchair reading the Business section
of The Sunday Times. Margaret is in her
preferred armchair reading the Styles
section. Denise, on the sofa, is reading the Book Review. Lorraine, sprawled
on the floor under Denise, reads the cartoon strip DONDI in the Daily News. Both
girls have changed from their Sunday
best to cotton blouses and pedal pushers.
Lorraine turns the page to the BRENDA
STARR comic strip where BRENDA is locked
in an embrace with the MYSTERY MAN.

                    DENISE
                (dreamily)
        I wonder what he'd look like…

                    LORRAINE
        Me too. Without that black eye
        patch.

                    DENISE
        Without those horn-rimmed glasses.

                    LORRAINE
                (looks up at Denise)
        What horn-rimmed glasses?

                        75

                    DENISE

Oh, never mind. You're going to
have to walk Bert Tuesdays after
school.

                    LORRAINE

How come?

                    DENISE

I have an extra extracurricular activity Tuesdays.

                    LORRAINE

Another one? How many do you need
to get into college?

                    DENISE

They're all in the arts. I need
something in the sciences. For
balance.

                    LORRAINE

So how are you going to pay me
back?

                    DENISE

The dishes. Wash, wipe and put away.

                    LORRAINE

No dice.

                    DENISE

Why not?

                    LORRAINE
Walking Bert takes more time than
the dishes.

                    DENISE
You drive a hard bargain. Okay.
I'll do the dishes Tuesday AND
Thursday.

                    LORRAINE
We-ll… It's a deal.

                    DENISE
Shake on it.

The girls shake hands, then finish off
their chocolate horns. There's a circum-
ference of chocolate around Lorraine's
mouth.

                    LEO
          (from behind his newspaper)
You people. You're going to get
pimples, you eat so much chocolate.

                    DENISE
Hmmm, I think I read somewhere that
ingesting too much sugar destroys
brain cells. Kind of like drinking
alcohol. Except it doesn't make you
drunk. Or maybe a different kind of
drunk.

                    LORRAINE

Daddy, you're the one who taught us
not to waste food. (quoting) "Every
grain of rice is a drop of sweat
from a Chinese peasant's brow."

                    DENISE

No wonder I don't like rice.

                     LEO

Chocolate isn't rice.

                   MARGARET

Don't forget we're going to Grampa's for dinner tonight.

                    LORRAINE

Why do I always have to wear a
dress to Grampa's? Crinolines are
so itchy.

                    DENISE
           (for MARGARET's ears only)

Why do Rainey and I have to go at
all? We can't understand a single
word, or anything else that's going
on.

                   MARGARET
            (to both daughters)

He's your grandfather. He gets to
see you only once a month. You want
to look nice for him.

                        DENISE
    ONLY!

                        LORRAINE
    It's so boring at Grampa's.

                        MARGARET
                (sympathetic, but anticipating
                LEO'S hard line)
    That's enough, young lady. You'll
    change into a clean dress for dinner.
    With a crinoline underneath. What
    kind of a mother will Grampa think I
    am if you look like a ragamuffin?

                        LEO
    Did you people finish your homework?

                        DENISE
    Everything except reading two chap-
    ters of *Tess of the d'Urbervilles*.

                        LEO
    You better read them before we
    leave.

                        DENISE
    But I always take some homework to
    Grampa's. What else is there for
    me to do? You and Grampa are always
    speaking Chinese.

    Margaret shoots Denise a cautionary look
    — too late.

                    LEO
          (throwing down the newspaper)
It's about time you people learned
Chinese. Then you'd know what Gram-
pa and I are talking about. And
you'd finally know something about
China.

                    MARGARET
I think you girls should go upstairs and finish your homework.

Sulking, Denise and Lorraine head up the
stairs.

                    LEO
If we lived in a Chinese neighborhood, your daughters would
know more about China. They'd be
speaking Chinese, reading Chinese,
thinking like a Chinese. Instead,
they're uneducated. Disrespectful.
(disdainfully) AMERICAN.

                    MARGARET
          (astutely leading him to her
          own conclusion)
Perhaps they'd be better educated
and more respectful if we lived in
Chinatown.

                    LEO

Are you crazy? So they could get
a job pushing a dim sum trolley in
some rat-infested restaurant on
Mott Street? So they could live in
New York City and not speak a word
of English? Is that the kind of future you want for your daughters?

Denise and Lorraine, who have been sitting at the top of the stairs all the
while, smile and nod at each other.

                    LEO

If it wasn't for me, you'd still be
making gowns for show business people in your mother's shop in Hell's
Kitchen.

                 MARGARET

You swept me off my feet. My most
ardent admirer. And a college boy
at that.

                    LEO

And you, you hadn't even finished
high school.

                 MARGARET
               (bristling)

I most certainly had. (proudly) I
passed my high school equivalen-
cy with flying colors. And that was

while I was also attending fashion design school. Mama wanted me
to have a set of skills so that I'd
never lack for a job.

                    LEO

Dressmaking! You call that a skill?

                 MARGARET

It's honest work. I've been told
I have excellent fashion sense. It
got me my job, didn't it?

                    LEO

Don't think I'm going to raise
a family of *le hu* — of entertain-
ers. Don't think that I don't know
that Lorraine tap dances in front
of the television like a puppet
on a string. Or that Denise sings
French songs like…like that skinny
woman always dressed in black with
a voice like a jackhammer…

                 MARGARET
              (somberly)

Edith Piaf. It's called vibrato.

                    LEO

Denise and Lorraine are going to
develop their minds. They're going
to go to college. Even get their
Ph.Ds. Become university professors.

                    MARGARET
          (dully)
I hope so, Leo. If that will make
you happy. And them.

                    LEO
What's HAPPINESS got to do with it?
It's their FUTURE I'm talking about.
And they're going to learn Chinese.
They wouldn't sit still and study
when I sent them to their grandfather's house to learn Chinese. Well,
they're two years older now. Take a
look at this.

Leo picks up the paper he threw down and
points to an advertisement.

                    LEO
Mandarin lessons. Audiotapes. Be-
ginner lessons. One through twenty.

Denise and Lorraine blanch. Their ex-
pressions are of both shock and dismay.
Bert, seated between them, licks first
Lorraine's mortified face, then Denise's.

                                        CUT

It was a seventy-minute drive to Lin Guoxin's home in Westchester County. The house, also a Dutch Tudor, was twice the size of Leo's, though its occupants numbered exactly one-half of Leo's family members (that is, before Prudie absconded): Lin Guoxin, Leo's father; Evelyn Lin, his second wife; and Aiying, their cook and housekeeper. To reach the manse, you left your car in a clearing about forty feet away from a hump-backed wooden bridge over a rushing stream which you had to cross in order to arrive at the home of the renowned Chinese calligrapher/poet/painter, once described in his own country as a national living treasure.

As the younger Lin family crossed the footbridge, Guoxin—erect and magisterial in his three-piece suit—and Evelyn—his much younger wife dressed in a silk cheongsam with a beaded cashmere sweater thrown casually over her shoulders—opened the front door and stepped out onto the patio. As Leo approached, Evelyn moved closer to her husband and slipped her hand into the crook of his arm. Leo greeted his father with a deferential nod. Though he was shorter by a good three inches, Guoxin seemed to tower above his son. Evelyn extended her hand to Leo in a way that suggested that the back of it should be kissed rather than the palm of it shaken. Refusing to do either, he acknowledged her with a stiff "Madam." Meanwhile, Margaret smiled politely and said demurely, "Ni hao," to both host and hostess. Evelyn nodded slightly in welcome, but

because Guoxin was busy pinching the cheeks of his two youngest granddaughters, he ignored Margaret's greeting. Whether he'd
heard it or pretended not to was open to question.

"*Lai, lai,*" Evelyn commanded softly.

Her guests filed into the foyer where Aiying took the box of
rugelach and the bottle of wine from Margaret and ushered everyone into the capacious living room decorated with Chinese antiques
and hanging landscape scrolls, many of them by Guoxin. The coffee
table was set with *zhongs* of Pu Er tea and dishes of sweetmeats
which Aiying would refill at appropriate intervals. In a corner of
the room, the black and white television set was turned on to the
evening news. The side tables were piled high with precariously
balanced Chinese newspapers and magazines. Leo and Guoxin sat
in the two armchairs that flanked the coffee table and conversed
in Mandarin. Evelyn sat in the third armchair she'd pulled close
to her husband's, hanging on his every word, offering him sweetmeats, picking imaginary lint off his lapel—in other words, trying
to distract him and interrupt his conversation with Leo. Margaret,
Denise, and Lorraine sat on the sofa behind the coffee table, which
the girls used to do their homework and where Margaret gratefully
rested her eyes when not scanning the other people in the room—
their attitudes, their facial expressions, their body language.

By the looks of things, the evening was no different from every
first Sunday evening of every month when the Lin juniors visited
the Lin seniors, except for Prudie's absence. But since Guoxin
hadn't inquired after her (though her absence was a gaping black
hole that had not eluded his detection), and since Leo (respectful of
or grateful for his father's withholding any comment on the matter,
or both) hadn't offered an explanation, the mental effort exerted by
everyone present to ensure a pleasant evening was greater, the mood
created by that mental effort blacker, the intention to lighten the

blacker mood created by their greater mental effort more in dead earnest—all of which prophesied a result diametrically opposed to the one they desired.

Guoxin, who every now and then had been casting inattentive glances at the television screen, suddenly pointed an emphatic finger at it.

"So this is what China has come to. A nation of peasants. What was once the center of the civilized world is now farmland growing thirty-pound cabbages and pigs the size of baby hippos."

Aiying appeared at the doorway separating the parlor from the dining room and caught Evelyn's eye.

"*Chi fan*," said the mistress of the house to her husband and stepson. "Let's go to dinner, shall we?" she said to Margaret, Denise, and Lorraine.

With a disgusted wave of her hand, she motioned Aiying to turn off the offending TV.

But the news program followed the Lins into the dining room where the rosewood table was set with a lazy susan offering dishes of braised mushrooms and baby bok-choy, roast duck, drunken chicken, steamed sea bass sprinkled with shredded ginger and scallions and bathed in soy sauce and sizzling hot oil, and gai-lan with oyster sauce. What ensued throughout the meal was a two-way conversation involving Leo and Guoxin revolving around China past and present.

"I might take issue with his methods," Leo said, the image of thirty-pound cabbages more visible in his mind than the flavor of the baby bok-choy in his mouth, "but Mao is rebuilding China after centuries of civil war and foreign imperialism."

Evelyn gave the lazy susan a spin, plucked the cheek—the tenderest morsel—of the sea bass with her chopsticks, and set it in her husband's bowl, though it was verifiably empty and he was audibly (two burps connoting satiation and satisfaction) full. He looked at the cheek disinterestedly. Everyone had avoided looking at Prudie's empty place at table.

"Not long ago," Leo continued, "China was called the sick man of Asia. Not anymore. Mao says China will outstrip England in steel production in five years. The United States in a decade."

"Is that supposed to reassure me of China's future greatness?" Guoxin picked up the fish cheek with his chopsticks, put it in his mouth, and scoffed, "Steel production!"

His displeasure seemed to be the signal for Evelyn to ring the small bell next to her wine glass. Its tinkle summoned Aiying, who appeared in scant seconds and cleared the table in not much more. After two whirlwind trips to and from the kitchen, she returned bearing a tray of rugelach.

"Ah, dessert!" Guoxin expelled.

What followed dessert was what always followed dinner at Guoxin's house: everyone retired to the piano room where they listened to Evelyn play a composition by one of the great Russian composers. Tonight the evening's entertainment was Rachmaninoff's *Piano Concerto No. 2.* At the piece's conclusion, everyone applauded politely except Guoxin, who had been moved to tears. When he took a white handkerchief from his jacket breast pocket and dabbed at his eyes, Evelyn's demeanor—self-possessed, aloof—underwent an instantaneous transformation. She *attacked* the piano with her hands, with her *entire body*, with a pent-up, explosive energy that belied her diminutive size.

"Stop! Stop!" Guoxin shouted, rising to his feet. "What is this? What are you playing?"

Leo and his family were shocked into silence. This was not another pleasant Sunday dinner like all other Sunday dinners at Guoxin's house.

Evelyn stopped playing and looked at her husband with glittering anthracite eyes.

"*Clair de Lune,*" she said, drily. "By Claude Debussy."

"No French composers. Or German composers. Or Italian composers." With each subsequent nationality, Guoxin's voice rose in both frequency and amplitude. "Or Austrian composers. In this house you will play music by Russian composers. Russian, and only Russian."

With clenched jaw, Evelyn played, thunderously, Rimsky-Korsakov's *Scheherazade.*

And thunder was what seemed imminent as the younger Lins took leave of their hosts. Not thunder, as in the weather. No, the night sky with its gibbous moon was cloudless; the humidity, low. But thunder nonetheless, not in the distant, gathering rumble preceding and announcing the violent eruption of driving wind, drenching rain, and blinding lightning. Thunder in the psychological sense, thunder in physiological and emotional terms. It began, as it always did, with hosts and guests congregating in the front vestibule and with Margaret turning to her daughters and saying, half-apologetically, half-confidentially:

"You girls…"

"Yes, we know," Denise and Lorraine said, simultaneously.

"…go to the car. Daddy and I will be along in a minute."

"C'mon, Den. It's the same old thing they don't want us to know about."

And why should they know about it, Margaret thought as they sauntered away, though they probably had an inkling of what that same old thing was. Every first Sunday for the past decade, the Lin dinners provided the opportunity for a family get-together and the pretext for the handoff (literally) of an envelope containing

Guoxin's next month's living expenses. In exchange for which, one might have expected some expression of his heartfelt gratitude and paternal love. But not in Guoxin's case. Quite the opposite. By now, Margaret had the Mutt and Jeff routine down pat. After the girls left, Leo stood before his father and addressed him formally. Though she didn't understand or speak Mandarin, Margaret surmised the gist of the dialogue through the men's gestures, body language, and facial expressions.

Leo: *Fuqin*, I hope you will allow me to fulfill a small portion of my obligation to you as your filial son… (He takes an envelope out of his pocket. Only tonight unlike previous nights, it is much thicker than usual.)

Guoxin: (feigning surprise) What is that? (Evelyn, at his side, moves even closer to her husband, Siamese twin-like.)

Leo: …by accepting this minuscule contribution to the management of your household. I am deeply ashamed that it is so paltry a sum, in no way commensurate with the debt that I owe you as your only son, the unworthy bearer of your illustrious name…

Guoxin: Is that (horrified) *money*?!

But tonight Leo goes off script. Judging by the thickness of the envelope, Margaret has deduced the reason even before Leo's admission.

Leo: (proudly) Double the usual amount. I sold my factory in Hong Kong.

Guoxin: So much the better. A businessman. A common merchant. As for your money, I have never requested such a consolation in exchange for my hopes and dreams for you.

Leo: (stung, struggling for self-composure) I cannot give you back your hopes and dreams, *fuqin*. It's too late for that. All I ask is that you accept what I *can* give you.

As on previous Sunday dinners, Leo extends the envelope to his father, who turns his head away and clasps his hands behind his back. Glorying in Leo's humiliation, Evelyn slides her hand into the crook of her husband's arm. Called upon to suffer in silence, to grin and bear it, Margaret takes a deep breath and sets her jaw for the *pièce de résistance*.

Guoxin: Dirty money! All money is tainted, but money obtained through trade and commerce is *filthy*.

It is here that walk-on Margaret becomes the protagonist, the pivot upon which the scene, if not the plot, turns. So deft is the maneuver—performed so often in the past—that it's barely visible to the naked eye and therefore questionable that it ever occurred. Margaret takes the envelope from Leo's hand and slips it into Guoxin's hands, still behind his back but unclasped, expectant. The thickness of the envelope makes the pupils of his eyes dilate. Margaret feels that the unreleased air in her lungs will cause them to explode if she doesn't expel it. But she holds it in. For now.

That night Margaret and Leo lay in bed awake, Leo's head and shoulders propped up on two pillows. The lamp on his night table was switched on and he smoked a cigarette while reading *The Wall Street Journal*. The newspaper had sat atop Lao Cao's most recent statement, which Leo had quickly placed face down. Things were looking up. His portfolio was doing well. Better than it had in years. The stock that Lao Cao had bought recently—Eddington Trading Corporation—was already reaping rewards. Rewards he didn't want Margaret to know about. Let *her* worry about finances for a change! He had, and long enough.

Margaret lay beside him staring at the ceiling. She reached for a tissue on her night table and sneezed into it, which forced her lungs to expel the remnants of whatever remained trapped in them at dinner.

"The envelope was thicker than usual."

"It contained a lot more money than usual. In fact, twice the amount."

Leo set the newspaper down on top of his stock report, turned off the light, and rolled over towards Margaret, who turned away, reached for another tissue, and sneezed into it. Leo rolled back to his side of the bed, turned the light back on, and pretended to continue reading the *Wall Street Journal*.

"I don't expect you to understand."

"Help me, Leo."

She turned over and lay on her back.

"Help me understand. Help me understand why your father won't sell any of his precious scrolls…" Her voice lowered in pitch but rose in volume. "…why instead he prefers to depend on you to support him and Evelyn. Help me understand why he makes a big production of refusing the money you give him very month only to accept it—behind his back—from me, humiliating you, demeaning me…"

"You're easily demeaned." Leo lowered the newspaper from in front of his face. "You've never complained about this before. Why now?"

"Leo, you're a filial son," Margaret said, changing tack. "But you have your own family to support. We need you as well. Our daughters' education. Their college funds. You said that a good portion of the money, if you decided to sell the factory, would go…"

"You forget there's one less daughter now." Leo turned out the light and lay on his back looking at the ceiling. "Besides, why should I worry about their college fund now that you're the breadwinner in the family? How much do you make, anyway, even with your promotion? Two hundred and fifty a week?" Leo turned over on his side, away from Margaret. "See what kind of college you can send them to on a salary like that."

Several minutes passed.

"They'd talk."

"They."

"People," Leo replied. "They'd say I'm a miser. 'The son of Lin Guoxin—Lin Guoxin, the renowned calligrapher—is a cheapskate.' Think how that would reflect on my father. On me. On all of us." Leo paused for Margaret's response but none was forthcoming. "My father always told me, 'With every privilege there comes responsibility. With every responsibility there comes privilege.' The law of reciprocity. If I have the privilege of being the son of Lin Guoxin, then I also have the responsibility that comes with it."

"Rights."

"What?"

"In America, we say rights. *Rights* and responsibilities," Margaret said. "Not privileges."

"Privileges. Rights. What's the difference?"

"Everything. Rights are innate, God-given. Privileges are granted by someone with more power to someone who has less.

"So they're the same thing. Your God gives you rights—and he's more powerful than you are."

Down the hallway, Denise and Lorraine also lay awake in bed having a conversation different in theme but similar in conclusion.

"Den. Den."

"What?" Denise answered irritably.

"How come Daddy always calls Madam Madam? Instead of her real name."

"Because he hates her."

"If I hated somebody, I could think of a lot worse names to call them than Madam."

"You don't understand. He hates her because she stole Grampa away from Nai-nai. Madam and Grampa never had any kids—she can't have any—so she tried to bribe Daddy with money when he was a boy into calling her Mama."

"What for?"

"So that Grampa would like her better. So she could wrap Grampa around her little finger."

"I don't get it. How could Daddy calling Madam Mama let her wrap Grampa around her little finger?"

"Forget it. Go to sleep."

"So does Daddy hate Grampa as well?"

"Of course not. Daddy's Grampa's son. He loves Grampa."

"How can you tell?"

"The same way you can tell that we love Daddy. Daddy wants to please Grampa. Just like we want to please Daddy. And even when we fail, we keep on trying."

"D'you think Prudie still loves Daddy? Do you think she stopped trying?"

"Go to sleep."

INT. BRONX HIGH SCHOOL OF SCIENCE -
TWO DAYS LATER

Denise and Douglas are in the ANIMAL LAB.
Douglas opens the door of a glass cage.
One SNAKE is inside it.

                    DOUGLAS
        First you get rid of the old straw…

He picks up the 1 1/2-foot snake.

                    DOUGLAS
        …careful not to throw the baby out
        with the bath water. Then you dump
        the old straw in that garbage can
        over there (gestures) and replace
        it with fresh straw from (gestures)
        that bin in the corner.

                    DENISE
        How much straw?

                    DOUGLAS
        Think Goldilocks. Not too much. Not
        too little. Just enough.

                    DENISE
        Where do you put the snake in the
        meantime?

> DOUGLAS
>
> We-ll, you can wear it as a turban
> (wraps snake around his head). As
> a scarf (wraps it around his neck
> and flings its tail over his shoul-
> der). As a noose (pulls the tail
> up, crosses his eyes, and hangs
> his tongue out of his mouth). Here,
> clasp your hands together like
> you're praying.

Denise complies. Douglas wraps the snake
around her wrists and forearms.

> DOUGLAS
>
> Voilà! Snakeskin handcuffs — the
> latest thing in serpentine fashion.

> DENISE
> (surprised)
>
> It feels cool and dry. Like plastic.

> DOUGLAS
>
> Bet you thought it would be wet and
> slimy, didn't you?

He opens another cage, takes out a SEC-
OND SNAKE and wraps it around her ankles.

> DENISE
>
> Hey, what are you doing?

> MR. EPSTEIN (O.S.)
>
> Alcock!

MR. EPSTEIN, the biology teacher — tall, balding and bearded — stands in the doorway.

> MR. EPSTEIN
> May I ask what's going on here? Or might I hazard a guess?

> DOUGLAS
> Oh, Mr. Epstein. I, um, I'm conducting a scientific experiment.

> MR. EPSTEIN
> (folding his arms across his chest)
> What sort of scientific experiment?

> DOUGLAS
> Man against beast, sir. Or, in this case, girl against beast. She's new to the animal lab. I'm testing her to see if she's suitable for the job.

Denise glares at Douglas.

> MR. EPSTEIN
> And who — that is, which — is the beast?

> DOUGLAS
> Why, the two snakes. You see, I'm trying to determine how long it'll take my assistant here to free

herself from their grip.

                    MR. EPSTEIN
And if she can't free herself,
which seems to be her current
predicament?

                    DOUGLAS
That's why, in scientific experi-
ments such as this, there's always
a control. That control, sir, is me
— should the strength of the snakes
be too great and she can't free
herself.

                    MR. EPSTEIN
It's reassuring to know that your
assistant is in such capable hands,
seeing that her own are tied.

                    DOUGLAS
Yes, Mr. Epstein.

                    MR. EPSTEIN
Would you mind untying them, Al-
cock? I think they're turning blue.
And her ankles too while you're at
it.

                    DOUGLAS
Yes, Mr. Epstein.

Douglas removes the two snakes, puts
them back in their cages. Denise rubs
her wrists.

> MR. EPSTEIN
>
> One more question, Alcock. Have you
> thought about what you want to ma-
> jor in at college?

> DOUGLAS
>
> Premed. I want to be a GP. That, or
> a vet.

> MR. EPSTEIN
>
> Is your father a general
> practitioner?

> DOUGLAS
>
> He's a trial lawyer.

> MR. EPSTEIN.
>
> Figures. And you, young lady? What
> do you want to be when you grow up?
> A snake charmer? Never mind.

Mr. Epstein leaves. Denise picks up a
WHITE MOUSE from inside a wire cage
and drops it down Douglas's shirt. He
shrieks, removes it, and puts it back in
its cage.

> DOUGLAS
> (blithering)
>
> You said you were afraid of mice!

                    DENISE
          You cured me.

          C.U. of the white mouse running round
          and round in its training wheel.

INT. NATURALIZATION & IMMIGRATION OFFICE -
DAY

          Hand over his heart, Leo stands in a
          large room with other soon-to-be cit-
          izens and recites the PLEDGE OF ALLE-
          GIANCE before the AMERICAN FLAG and an
          IMMIGRATION OFFICER.

                    IMMIGRATION OFFICER
          Congratulations, everyone. You are
          now citizens of the greatest coun-
          try in the world. The United States
          of America.

          All but Leo — who looks DAZED — shake
          hands, slap each other on the back, hug
          each other, etc. One EUROPEAN MAN grabs
          Leo by the shoulders and kisses him on
          both cheeks.

INT. LIN HOUSE - DAY — WEEKS LATER

          Leo stands in the middle of Prudie's
          room, mop, pail, broom, dustpan, and
          rags in hand. He looks around, admiring

his handiwork. The room is SPOTLESS and
spartan, scoured of anything that smacks
of Prudie. Across the hall, in Denise
and Lorraine's CLUTTERED and messy room,
the two girls are sprawled on their re-
spective beds. A reel-to-reel TAPE RE-
CORDER plays a Chinese language lesson.
They repeat in bored monotone voices the
words they hear on the tape.

> TAPE
>
> *Wo hui shuo zhongguo hua.* [I can
> speak Chinese.]

> DENISE AND LORRAINE
> (simultaneously)
>
> *Wo hui shuo zhongguo hua.* [I can
> speak Chinese.]

Leo opens their door without knocking.

> LEO
>
> You people. Come with me.

> DENISE
>
> Right now? Where?

> LEO
>
> Hurry up.

> DENISE
>
> I've got lots of homework, and to-
> morrow we're having a big test in…

                    LEO

Bring your homework with you. You
can study at the airport.

                  LORRAINE

   Airport?

                    LEO

And don't forget to turn off the
tape recorder.

Leo heads down the stairs. Denise and
Lorraine turn off the tape recorder and
gather up their books. They stop and
peer into Prudie's pristine room.

                  LORRAINE
                 (whispers)

D'you think Prudie's coming home?

                   DENISE

Rats! There goes my all-to-myself
bedroom.

SOUND OF A JET LANDING.

INT. IDLEWILD AIRPORT — TWO HOURS LATER

C.U. of SIGN "Gate 15." SOUND OF JET EN-
GINE FADES. We see people rushing about.
Leo paces back and forth. In the waiting
area, Lorraine and Denise are slumped in
their seats, half-asleep.

LOUDSPEAKER (O.S.)

Ladies and gentlemen. Flight number
31 from Havana, Cuba has just arrived at gate number 15. Passengers
will begin deplaning momentarily.

LORRAINE
(jolted awake)

Gee! Prudie went to Cuba?

DENISE
(roused from her slumber)

Naw, I don't think so — not unless
she and her husband went to pay
Nai-nai a visit. (sits bolt upright) Uh-oh.

M.S. of NAI-NAI — tiny CHINESE WOMAN in
her early 70s — wanders through Gate 15.
She looks disoriented, bewildered. Denise stares at her with foreboding.

DENISE (O.S.)

Prudie didn't go to Cuba. And she's
not coming back home to live with
us. Nai-nai is.

LORRAINE (O.S.)

Nai-nai! Really? I wonder what
she's like.

>   DENISE

Really old. Really short. Fun-
ny-looking. A pie face and round
wire-rimmed glasses and a weird
dress that makes her look like a
100-pound sack of rice. (under her
breath) And to think she's getting
MY bedroom!

>   LORRAINE

How d'you know?

>   DENISE
>   (juts her chin in NAI-NAI'S di-
>   rection)

Take a look.

>   LORRAINE
>   (craning her neck)

That old lady with the tea cozy on
her head?

Close to tears, Nai-nai scurries to Leo,
beams at him, pats his arms with both
her hands as if she can't believe he is
real. Leo nods and smiles at her.

>   LEO

Mama.

>   NAI-NAI
>   (in Mandarin)

Ten years. It's been ten years.

Leo leads her by the hand over to Denise
and Lorraine. They both come to their
feet.

                    LEO
    What do you people say? Say 'ni
    hao' to your Nai-nai. (to DENISE)
    You don't remember your grandmother.
    You were too young. And you (to
    LORRAINE) weren't even born yet.

              DENISE AND LORRAINE
                (simultaneously)
    Ni hao, Nai-nai.

                  NAI-NAI
              (smiling broadly)
    (to DENISE) Plu-dee. (to LORRAINE)
    Duh-nee-zah.

                  LORRAINE
            (whispering to DENISE)
    She's got gold-rimmed teeth.

                    LEO
              (in Mandarin)
    No, Mama. Denise and Lorraine. The
    middle daughter and the youngest.
    Prudie is away at college — far
    away, in California.

                    NAI-NAI
               (looks at DENISE)

     Oh. Duh-nee-zuh. (looks at LOR-
     RAINE) Law-lane.

     Nai-nai pulls a tiny AMERICAN FLAG out
     of her handbag and waves it.

                    NAI-NAI
     A-mell-i-ka.

     Denise and Lorraine manage wan smiles.

INT. AIRPORT PHONE BOOTH - MINUTES LATER

     Leo is on the phone. Nai-nai, Denise,
     and Lorraine wait outside the booth with
     Nai-nai's luggage.

                    LEO
     I thought you'd be home by now.
     I tried calling you. No answer.

INT. SAKS FIFTH AVENUE

     Margaret is at her desk, which is inun-
     dated with SHOES, HATS, GLOVES, JEWELRY.
     The cork board behind her is push-pinned
     with scores of pages from VOGUE, L'OFFI-
     CIEL, HARPER'S BAZAAR magazines, fashion
     photos, head shots of models, etc.

> MARGARET
>
> I thought I would've been home by
> now too, but I'm doing double-duty.
> One of my assistants was sick and
> went home, so I…

INT. AIRPORT PHONE BOOTH

> LEO
>
> You seem to be spending a lot more
> time at work these days. Nai-nai's
> plane landed. The girls and I just
> got her luggage. We'll be home in
> an hour or so, if we don't hit
> traffic.

INT. SAKS FIFTH AVENUE

> MARGARET
>
> I think I can finish up in the next
> twenty minutes. Half an hour at
> the most. You'll make it home be-
> fore I do. I wish I could be there,
> to welcome Nai-nai and all. I'd
> planned on it. If it weren't for my
> assistant not feeling well…

INT. AIRPORT PHONE BOOTH

> LEO
>
> I just called to tell you to take
> a taxi home. I won't be coming to
> pick you up at the subway station.

INT. SAKS FIFTH AVENUE

                    MARGARET
        Of course. I'll take a taxi.

INT. AIRPORT PHONE BOOTH

                    LEO
        I have to go. They're waiting for
        me.

INT. SAKS FIFTH AVENUE

        Margaret is about to say something when
        she hears a CLICK, then DIAL TONE. With
        a sigh, she hangs up the phone, which
        immediately rings. She picks it up
        eagerly.

                    MARGARET
        Hello? (pause) Oh, it's you. (looks
        around to see if anyone is lis-
        tening, lowers her voice) No, of
        course not. I just thought it was
        someone else. (pause) Oh, I'd love
        to, but I can't. Not this evening.
        Of course I understand it's on
        the spur of the moment — our meet-
        ings have to be. (pause) No, ev-
        erything's fine. We'll get together
        another time. Soon. Very soon. I
        promise.

Margaret hangs up.

FADE OUT

Thanks to heavy traffic from south Queens to the north Bronx, and luck in catching the express train, Margaret arrived a mere seven minutes after Leo. She'd have been the first to admit that she was not a good cook—even less so, now that she was a working woman. That morning, she'd taken the chicken legs and thighs out of the freezer to defrost. With the addition of boiling water, dehydrated flakes from a box would coagulate into mashed potatoes in seconds. Employing the same method, string beans—frozen, also from a box—would become edible. For dessert (served in the Lin house only on special occasions): store-bought Dutch apple pie à la mode with vanilla ice cream.

"Welcome, welcome," Margaret said to—and Leo translated for—her mother-in-law. "I'm sorry I wasn't here to give you a proper welcome. Welcome to the United States, to our home, which is now yours. We hope you'll be very happy with us."

Margaret then set to work. She slipped an apron over her elegant ensemble not to lose any precious time getting dinner on the table and suggested (through Leo) that Nai-nai go to her room and rest after the long flight from Cuba. But the old woman's expression and gestures indicated that no, she was fine, she'd remain in the kitchen, out of the way, please pay no attention to her.

Curious, attentive, Nai-nai looked on as Margaret dredged the chicken pieces in flour and placed them in a skillet of sizzling cooking oil, turning them every few minutes. She watched her tear the carton from the frozen string beans and dump them into a pot of boiling water, then pour boiling water from a kettle into a large bowl of white flakes which, when whipped with a fork, became instantaneously a white paste that looked a bit like *juk*—rice porridge—only thicker. More like cement before it hardened. When the chicken pieces had darkened to a medium brown, Margaret removed them from the skillet and placed them on paper towels which immediately became an oil slick. She turned up the flame under the skillet and added flour and canned chicken broth to the remaining cooking oil and bits of crust that had failed to adhere to the chicken and instead stuck to the pan. As she stirred it, the mixture bubbled and thickened into gravy of—to Nai-nai's eyes at least—a rather unappetizing hue. Margaret placed the chicken pieces on a large platter which Denise carried to the dining room table, followed by Lorraine carrying the bowl of mashed potatoes, followed by Margaret, a sauceboat of gravy in one hand and a bowl of string beans in the other.

"*Chi fan*," Leo announced, surrendering his usual place at table to his mother and taking his seat to her right, formerly Margaret's, who now sat to Nai-nai's left.

"*A table*," Denise murmured under her breath.

Lorraine made a quick Sign of the Cross.

Bert sat on the floor next to Nai-nai's chair, whimpering to gain her attention and sympathy. Leo silenced him with a look. Margaret plopped a mound of mashed potatoes on her mother-in-law's plate. Using the bowl of the gravy ladle, she made a crater which she filled with the slow-moving, dun-colored liquid from the sauceboat which overflowed, congealing instantly on the plate. The mini-volcano and its erupting lava were soon joined by a chicken leg and thigh encased in a thick crust glistening with grease, and finally a generous helping of string beans boiled to a wan green-gray and drowning in butter. To prepare for the gustatory experience ahead, Nai-nai fortified herself with a sip from her water glass before taking knife and fork in hand.

Though far more experienced with chopsticks, she was ready to do battle with Western food using Western weapons. She who had survived plague, famine, war, and revolution could surely survive American food as well.

Survive her first American dinner Nai-nai did, and with admirable dignity and forbearance. It was, however, an experience she'd rather not repeat. More than herself, it was her granddaughters she was thinking of. Their health. Their wellbeing. What kind of food came out of a box? Was it food at all? And chicken should be fresh-killed, just plucked, still warm from the chopping block. Not hard as a rock, pulled from a tomb of ice in which it had lain mummified for days, perhaps weeks.

But how could she accomplish her goal of feeding her family real food, healthful food, *delicious* food and do so while maintaining her own face and saving that of her daughter-in-law? Might she, say, take over the kitchen without usurping Margaret's position as mistress of the rest of the house? Clearly, the kitchen was the one room over which her daughter-in-law had no wish (or right) to reign. Margaret was a working woman. Out of the house from nine to five. Some days, Leo told his mother, even later. Much later. Might Margaret consider delegating the responsibilities associated with making dinner for her family to me, Nai-nai suggested to her son.

"I would consider it a privilege. Not only a privilege, but I'd be able to both contribute to the family's welfare and feel I'm being useful. It would give me a purpose as well as great pleasure—something to do with my time, something I would enjoy doing. Do you think Margaret would grant me this favor? I would be forever indebted to her."

How could Margaret refuse when the request, made though Leo, was put this way?

Her voice said, tentatively, I suppose, if that's what she wishes. But her eyes said, immediately, YES! BY ALL MEANS, YES!

One mission accomplished, Nai-nai requested that Leo take her on a tour of the front yard, bisected into two stretches of lawn by a flagstone path, each portion of lawn bordered by flowerbeds in bloom. Tulips, daffodils, hyacinths, jonquils grew in one. In the other, voluptuous pink and white peony bushes and dainty lily of the valley encircled the two *ailanthus altissima* trees whose abundant pollen was the principal cause of Margaret's olfactory distress. Having lived in Guilin, Hong Kong, and Cuba, where she'd been surrounded by orchids, birds of paradise, jasmine, hibiscus, palmetto palms, banyan trees, and osmanthus trees, Nai-nai was unimpressed by Margaret's flowerbeds and horrified by the two Chinese sumac trees that stank to high heaven—for that was the only "heaven" applicable to them and not their appellation Tree of Heaven. She spent no time dwelling on the superiority of her past gardens but envisioned what she might plant in the present one— not for their aesthetic value but for practical purposes: economic and nutritional. Round red globes of tomatoes would supplant the tulips, hyacinths, jonquils, and daffodils. In deference to Margaret's love of lilies of the valley and her own preference for peonies, she'd leave that particular garden untouched and set her botanical sights, her hoe, and her trowel on her granddaughters' backyard sandbox, unused for years. Instead of the long-abandoned swing set, teeter-totter and slide, rows of bok-choy, bumpy string beans, gai-lan, and bitter melon. As for the "ledge," as her granddaughters called it—a wilderness of brambles, tall grasses, and wild blackberry bushes inundating a plateau separated from the small backyard hill by a five-foot stone outcropping—she would repeat the horticultural bounty she planned for the sandbox garden.

Final stop on the tour was the garage. Currently, it housed Katrinka, a lawnmower, ladders, buckets, ropes, cans of paint, and gardening tools. In their place, she imagined cage upon cage of clucking, squawking chickens. Live, *very live*, chickens. She broke into a smile, into a grin, into a closed-lipped chuckle, and finally into a wide-open-mouthed, gold-teeth-baring cackle of pure delight to hear all those imaginary birds cackling along with her.

Margaret was perfectly amenable to the idea that her flower beds—which, being a working woman, she could no longer take proper care of—would be transformed into Nai-nai's vegetable gardens. (As for Denise and Lorraine, they had no say regarding the future use of their childhood sandbox and ledge.) Nai-nai's suggestion that the garage be transformed into a chicken farm, however, did not sit well with Leo, who was quick to find a solution: a Chinese man living in Yonkers who'd had the same idea as his mother. Thereafter, once or twice a week, Leo drove Nai-nai— and sometimes Denise, or Lorraine, or both—to the fowl farm to supply her with the fresh-killed chickens she insisted upon.

Today had been such a day.

Seated in the front passenger seat, cradling the butcher-paper-packaged remains of two hens still warm from the chopping block, Nai-nai stuck her arm out the window.

"Stop! Stop!"

Leo brought Katrinka to an abrupt halt. "What's the matter?"

"Gow-gay," she said, pointing emphatically to the bushes growing on one of the medians dividing Cranston Road. Before he could stop her, she opened the car door and trundled towards one of the bushes which she fondled with almost erotic pleasure. "Gow-gay. Don't you recognize it? It was your favorite soup when you were a boy." She peeled off her cardigan and began filling it, sack-like, with gow-gay leaves.

Sunlight glinted off her gold-rimmed teeth exposed in a rapturous grin. Hearing a car approaching, Denise and Lorraine sank down in the back seat until it drove by.

"How do you like that!" Leo murmured. "To think that gow-gay grows on the street where we live."

"The girls are in for a treat," Nai-nai said, pulling off leaves by the handful. "I'll make gow-gay soup tonight with beaten egg."

"That's enough. That's plenty. Come back to the car."

"It's barely enough for tonight."

"Don't worry about that. There'll be fewer of us for dinner. Margaret's working late tonight," Leo explained, an edge to his voice. "She'll be eating at work."

"But the growing season for gow-gay is so short. Soon the leaves will be bitter."

"Denise and Lorraine will bring you back here on the weekend. They'll help you pick all the gow-gay you want."

Denise and Lorraine looked at each other grimly, their comprehension of spoken Mandarin adequate enough to have understood the gist of their father's words.

Satisfied with such an arrangement, Nai-nai tied the sleeves of her cardigan together to form a bundle and got back into the car. At home, she no sooner entered the house than she headed back out—to her heaven on earth, her sanctuary, her Elysian fields: her vegetable gardens. The sun was starting to set, the perfect time to water and fertilize her plants and settle them in for the night.

Denise was also no sooner in the house than she headed back out as well—Bert on his leash in one hand and a covered pail and a trowel in the other. This was the least favorite of her daily chores, one occasioned by two facts—Prudie had flown the coop and their grandmother ruled the roost. Both required that she return from walking the dog bearing a pail filled with his excrement and urine.

"*Xie-xie,*" Nai-nai said when Denise entered the sandbox and handed her the pail. "*Two* kinds of fertilizer," she emphasized so that her granddaughter would appreciate the rationale for and the results of her request, "to make my vegetables taste *twice* as good!"

She spread Bert's bounty around her plants and decided not to water them. She didn't even have to look up at the sky to know what kind of night it would be. She could tell by the breeze, the smell and feel of the air. Tonight the breeze would turn into wind. A strong wind. And it would rain. It would rain very hard.

That evening, after a nearly silent dinner—gow-gay soup, see-yao gai chicken, diced pork sautéed with bitter melon, gai-lan in oyster sauce, and boiled white rice—except for a few words between mother and son regarding the dinner itself, Leo retired to the master bedroom to read the evening papers and enjoy a smoke. He'd left the door open.

Their homework completed, Denise and Lorraine lolled on their beds and listened to Mandarin language tapes whose words and sentences they repeated simultaneously in nasal monotone voices. Their door was also open.

Nai-nai was seated in the armchair in her (formerly Prudie's) bedroom patching a *siming* blanket. The door was shut.

The house was completely quiet except for the tape recorder playing at low volume. Everyone was upstairs except for Bert who was seated on the back of his armchair looking out the window at the gathering storm clouds. A flicker of lightning followed by a rumble of thunder drove him from his favorite spot. As he raced up the stairs, the phone rang.

"There's Mom," Lorraine concluded, cuddling Bert, who'd taken refuge on her bed.

The language tape droned on. The telephone continued to ring. Why didn't their father pick up the receiver? At least half a minute elapsed before the ringing stopped, but not because Leo had answered the phone. If he had, his daughters, who'd turned off the tape recorder, would have heard him telling their mother that he'd pick her up at the station.

The phone rang again. And it kept ringing. Lorraine jumped up off her bed just as another flash of lightning, brighter than the last, illuminated the bedroom window, throwing momentary silhouettes of the sumac's leaves and branches onto the venetian blinds. The storm was coming closer; the peals of thunder were longer, louder.

"Where are you going? We haven't finished our lesson yet."

But Lorraine, Bert at her heels, was already out the door and heading for the master bedroom. She stood in the doorway—looking at her father, waiting, anticipating—where she was soon joined by Denise. The phone continued to ring on the night table inches away from where Leo lay, half-supine, his back propped up against two pillows. He raised his eyes from the newspaper he was reading and acknowledged his daughters with a disinterested, "What is it?"

"That's Mom," Denise said, nodding at the phone, which was still ringing.

"I hear it," Leo said, too calmly.

When Bert squirmed between Lorraine's legs and jumped up on the bed, Leo shoved him onto the floor.

"C'mere, Bert. Come on, boy," Lorraine encouraged, arms outstretched and taking a few tentative steps into the room.

"Why don't you answer it?" Denise asked, following her sister into the room.

"I told you. That dog is not allowed on my bed. Don't you people understand English? And close the door on your way out."

Instead, Denise walked over to the night stand.

"Don't touch that."

Lorraine burst into tears.

"That's Mom calling," Denise said, her voice wavering between fear and anger. "Why aren't you leaving to pick her up at the station?"

The phone stopped ringing. Lorraine stopped crying. All three eyed it suspiciously, expectantly, until Leo broke the breathless silence. "Go back to your room." When they hesitated, he added, "Don't make me repeat myself."

Denise and Lorraine sat on the edge of their beds listening to the whistling of the wind, the drumming of the rain, the roar and rumble of thunder, the creak and whine of the swaying branches of the sumac trees, the scratching of twigs, like arthritic fingers, at their bedroom window. When the back doorbell rang, they jumped to their feet and raced down the stairs, Bert leading the way.

"Mommy!" Lorraine cried out.

But it was their father who loomed out of the shadows and stood in front of the back door. (How long had he been standing there, anticipating Margaret's arrival, and that of his daughters?)

"Go back to your room."

Denise and Lorraine remained rooted in place, both petrified by fear and defiant of his command. The buzzer sounded again. Longer. More insistent. It stopped when Margaret began frantically knocking on the door. Bert yowled and Leo gave him a swift kick in the ribs.

"Don't!" Denise shouted, glaring at her father, kneeling to take Bert, whimpering, into her arms.

The dog yelped again, this time when there was another crack and boom of thunder. Denise held him tighter, stifling the urge to cry.

"Leo," came a plaintive voice from the other side of the door. "Leo, open the door."

"Please, Daddy," Lorraine begged, on the verge of tears. "Please open the door."

"Please, Leo," the small voice came again. "Let me in."

"Mama! Mama!" Lorraine bawled, snot and tears running down her face.

Nai-nai appeared in the back hallway. "What's happening?"

"Go back to bed, Mama."

"Why is Lorraine crying?" she asked baffled, concerned. "Is she sick?"

"Go back to bed, I said."

"Leo. Leo, please," the voice sobbed, the fists pounded less forcefully, more hopelessly. "Open the door."

Stupefied, Nai-nai stared at her son. "That's Margaret."

"Do as I say!" Leo exploded. "Go back upstairs!"

Nai-nai flinched as if she had been struck, lowered her eyes, and headed back up the stairs. Ashamed and drained by his outburst, Leo slumped bonelessly against the back door.

"Mommy! Mommy!" Lorraine called, running to the front door. She unlocked it, flung it open wide, and raced out into the lashing rain. "Mommy! Mommy!" she yelled over the crashing thunder.

Denise and Bert followed her and stood just outside the doorway. Frequent flashes of lightning illuminated Lorraine and Margaret, both of them soaked through, clutching each other, sobbing as they walk up the flagstone path towards the front steps. Denise turned on the entrance lamps on either side of the door. Despite the storm, the claps of thunder, Denise could hear their voices clearly, though their figures were obscured or distorted by billowing curtains of wind-swept rain—her mother's, somber but reassuring; her sister's, frightened but relieved:

"I'm scared, Mama. I'm scared."

"Don't be. It's all over now. It's all over."

INT. DENISE AND LORRAINE'S BEDROOM —
20 MINUTES LATER

The entire scene is one long shot of the
VENETIAN BLIND with silhouettes of the
sumac tree branches whipping about wild-
ly in a *danse macabre* on an otherwise
white background. Later, they transform
into vivid images of what Denise envi-
sions. Sound of WIND, RAIN and THUNDER.

                    LORRAINE (O.S.)
          I can't fall asleep.

                    DENISE (O.S.)
          Then you should watch the movie.

SOUND of rustling sheets.

                    LORRAINE (O.S.)
          Movie? What are you talking about?

                    DENISE (O.S.)
          The venetian blind. On my side of
          the room.

                    LORRAINE (O.S.)
          That's just a window. With branches
          waving around making shadows.

                    DENISE (O.S.)   —
          Look longer. Through half-closed
          eyes. (pause) Well? What do you see?

                    LORRAINE (O.S.)
          Branches. What do YOU see?

          The waving branches become VIVID IMAGES
          starting now.

                    DENISE (O.S.)
          A man. Walking.

                    LORRAINE (O.S)
          Where?

                    DENISE (O.S.)
          He's stopping. He's sitting down.

                    LORRAINE (O.S.)
          I don't see any of that.

                    DENISE (O.S.)
          He just pulled his knees up to his
          chin. Wait a minute. It's not a man.
          It's a GIANT. And somebody a lot
          smaller — a normal human being — is
          walking up the giant's back.

          SOUND of rustling sheets.

                    LORRAINE (O.S.)
          You're making this up.

                    DENISE (O.S.)
     Am not. She's carrying a sack.
     Filled with something. It's heavy.

                    LORRAINE (O.S.)
     How d'you know it's a she?

                    DENISE (O.S.)
     By the way she swung the sack
     over her other shoulder. She'd
     just switched shoulders. The sack
     wouldn't be heavy for a boy.

The WIND, RAIN and THUNDER stop. The BRANCH-
ES are still.

                    LORRAINE (O.S.)
                (sleepily)
     What's in the sack?

                    DENISE (O.S.)
     I have no idea. The movie stopped.

                    LORRAINE (O.S.)
     Before the end? That's not a movie.
     That's a dream. Dreams always end
     right before they give you the an-
     swer you've been waiting for. In-
     stead, you wake up.

RUSTLE of sheets. SOUND OF Lorraine
yawning loudly. The silhouettes of the
sumac branches on the venetian blind are
deathly still.

                    LORRAINE (O.S.)
'Nite.

                     DENISE (O.S.)
'Nite. (sighs) I wish we could still
watch Winky Dink and You. All you
had to do was connect the dots with
a Magic Crayon and you knew what
was what. A lion cage. A bridge.
Don't you, Rainey?

The SOUND of Rainey's heavy breathing.

                                        CUT

Rake in hand, Leo stood in the front yard surveying the previous night's damage. Leaves and twigs littered the lawn. The peony bushes had been beaten senseless to the ground and a large branch, ripped from one of the sumac trees, lay on its side like a huge felled prey. Leo walked over to the monstrous limb and put one foot on it as if it were a hunting trophy, a wild animal he'd had in his sites and finally brought down.

Miraculously, Nai-nai's front yard vegetable garden escaped the storm's wrath: a few squashed tomatoes and one or two listing tomato plants, thanks to the stakes she'd plunged deep into the ground and tied them to. She glanced at Leo, the fallen branch.

"It's a good thing that didn't land on the house," she remarked, adding, "or anyone."

"They have to be cut back," Leo said, referring to the sumac trees. "This wouldn't have happened if I'd trimmed the branches. I'm surprised more didn't come down. A clean break," he noted, inspecting the fatality. "It just snapped."

Nai-nai approached and plucked one of the sumac flowers which she twirled between her thumb and forefinger.

"Poor Margaret! Always sneezing—and all because of this. Such a little thing. Such a big effect. She'll be so happy when you cut back the branches. You'll be saving her nose." Involuntarily she thought: And who knows what else.

The following Saturday, an undercurrent of excitement ran though the Lin residence. Denise and Lorraine both felt it had something to do with the night of the big storm although—or because—the feeling was the diametrical opposite of what they'd felt that night. It was the two sisters who felt the electricity most intensely, though it was their parents who were going out for dinner and dancing. Margaret, who'd chosen to wear a cream-colored silk brocade cocktail dress with Chinese accents, sat calmly at her vanity table brushing her hair while Lorraine rummaged through her mother's jewelry box. Seated at her father's desk and out of her mother's and sister's view, Denise pilfered two cigarettes from the pack of Kents in the top drawer and slid them into her skirt pocket.

"Wear these, Mom," Lorraine suggested, holding up a pair of gold and pearl clip-ons. "Here, let me do it."

"Well, what do you think?" Margaret, earrings in place, turned and asked Denise.

"You're beautiful," Lorraine decided, enchanted.

"It's hard to imagine you and Daddy going out dancing," Denise said. "You, yes. But Daddy!"

"Actually, your father's a very good dancer."

"I didn't know that," Lorraine said as she searched for more buried treasure in her mother's dresser drawer.

Margaret looked at her reflection in the vanity mirror, tugged at the earrings (which pinched a bit but then what wouldn't one do for appearances' sake?), and smiled wistfully.

"There are a lot of things you don't know about your father."

"Like what?" Denise asked.

"What's this?" Lorraine held up an oval cream-colored object the size of a baby's fist. "Where did you find that?" Margaret took it from Lorraine and brought it close to her eyes. She studied it, turned it over and over in her hand. Her rapt attention drew Denise to her side.

"From the little jewelry box in your dresser drawer," Lorraine replied. "Under a lot of other stuff."

"I'd forgotten all about it. Daddy gave it to me. Years ago. It's white jade. The kind Chinese call mutton-fat. Because of the color. Tongue of jade."

"Neat," Denise said, taking it. "It really *is* the size and shape of a tongue. A thick tongue. What's this carved on it?"

"It's meant to look like a cicada."

"What's a cicada?" Lorraine asked.

"A very fat grasshopper." Denise placed the gemstone in Lorraine's hand. "See the wings?"

"Your father told me a story about it when he gave it to me. He said the ancient Chinese buried their dead with a piece of jade. They believed it prevented the body from decaying. For them, the cicada was a symbol of immortality. For example, see that piece of jade in your hand? It would be placed in the dead person's mouth—a tongue of jade—so he could speak to the living from beyond the grave."

"Ee-yew! That's really yucky!"

"No yuckier than placing the body of Christ in your mouth during Holy Communion."

"Mom," Lorraine moaned, "tell her to stop!"

"Denise," Margaret chided gently.

"Tell her that's a sacrilege what she just said. Tell her that's a sin."

"I can't wait till you're in sixth grade and the nuns make you wear those Lisle stockings the color of Calamine lotion," Denise said, narrowing her eyes. "Even when it's summer. And to hold them up, that instrument of torture—a garter belt that always twists around your waist and leaves red marks and indentations on your thighs."

Katrinka honked, putting an abrupt end to the impending argument that Margaret had no desire to mediate. And now, no time. She rose from the vanity and walked to the bed to pick up her matching opera coat, beaded clutch, and elbow-length kidskin gloves lying there. A second, longer, shriller blast from Katrinka pulled Margaret to the front door. She turned momentarily to remind Denise who, together with Lorraine, had followed her down the stairs:

"When you walk Bert, don't forget to…"

"I won't…" Denise answered brightly, then when her mother crossed the threshold out of earshot, she concluded through gritted teeth, "…turn into some goddamn Chinese peasant carrying goddamn pails of night soil to fertilize Nai-nai's goddamn vegetables. Just see if you can make me."

Lorraine walked to the living room window and stood beside Bert, sitting in his favorite spot, and gazed out the window. Her mother hurried down the flagstone path not to keep her father—scowling, tapping his foot impatiently—waiting any longer. Then she watched as her mother glided effortlessly to the car where Leo, dressed in white tie and tails, tipped his top hat and opened the door for her with an elegant flourish. As for Margaret, she matched him in glamour and charm, having instantaneously traded her brocade cocktail dress—thanks to the indelible image of Fred Astaire and Ginger Rogers in *Top Hat* recently burned into Lorraine's memory—for a pale silk chiffon gown, its sleeves and hem fluttering with marabou. She didn't walk but floated down the path and drifted into the front seat like an ethereal cloud. Leo executed a few feather-light dance steps and closed the car door with a suave kick of his patent-leathered, tap-dancing foot. Katrinka backed down the driveway, but in Lorraine's eyes the family car was a Rolls-Royce gliding along Park Avenue.

INT. ST. AGATHA'S SCHOOL - DAY

In the school lunchroom Lorraine opens
her lunch box and starts to eat the
STEAMED PORK BUN inside. When two CLASS-
MATES approach, she wolfs it down and
quickly shuts her lunch box. The CLASS-
MATES sit down at her table. The FIRST
CLASSMATE opens his lunch box and in-
spects his sandwich.

> FIRST CLASSMATE
>
> Baloney.

> SECOND CLASSMATE
>
> I did so get 92 on my arithmetic
> test. Wanna see? Here, I'll prove
> it to you.

She pulls out a sheet of paper and
thrusts it under First Classmate's eyes.

> FIRST CLASSMATE
>
> I meant baloney. My mom made me
> my favorite sandwich. Baloney and
> American cheese. With lots of may-
> onnaise and iceberg lettuce.

> SECOND CLASSMATE
> (opening her lunch box)
>
> Look what I got for dessert.
> Twinkies. Two of 'em. How 'bout
> you?

                          FIRST CLASSMATE
Chuckles.

                          SECOND CLASSMATE
I'll trade you one of my Twinkies
for three of your Chuckles. You can
even keep the black one.

                          FIRST CLASSMATE
                        (to LORRAINE)
What d'you got for dessert?

                          LORRAINE
Nothing.

                          SECOND CLASSMATE
You gotta have dessert. No dessert
is…is…un-American.

First Classmate flips open the lid on
Lorraine's lunchbox.

                          LORRAINE
Hey!

First and Second Classmates look inside.
Each picks up something small wrapped in
paper.

                          FIRST CLASSMATE
And you said you didn't have
dessert!

                          LORRAINE
              Give them back!

          She grabs at them both.

                          LORRAINE
              I'll call the lunchroom monitor.

                        SECOND CLASSMATE
              What are they?

                          LORRAINE
                        (folding her arms over her
                        chest)
              Can't you read?

                        FIRST CLASSMATE
                        (studying the wrapper)
              Not this I can't.

                          LORRAINE
                        (superior)
              Didn't think so. It's Chinese. I've
              been studying Chinese…

          Lorraine takes the packet of dried beef
          away from First Classmate.

                          LORRAINE
              …ever since my Chinese grandmother
              came to live with us. I'll tell you
              what it says. (scrutinizing the
              wrapper) Tree bark. From the Chi-
              nese elm tree.

                    SECOND CLASSMATE
You mean Dutch elm. We have one
growing in our front…

                        LORRAINE
How can a DUTCH elm grow in China?
No, I mean a CHINESE elm.

Lorraine tears open the packet of dried
beef and holds up the DRIED BEEF inside.

                        LORRAINE
See? Chinese elm bark.

                    SECOND CLASSMATE
                (taking it from LORRAINE)
Let me see. Looks kinda like tree
bark.

Lorraine reclaims the dried beef, tears
off a piece, pops it in her mouth.

                     FIRST CLASSMATE
Yeuch! Are you crazy?

                        LORRAINE
                (gives the rest to SECOND
                CLASSMATE)
Here, I dare you to eat a piece.

Second Classmate shakes her head.

>   LORRAINE
>   What's the matter? Afraid you'll
>   grow a twig in your stomach?

First Classmate gingerly opens his packet, screams, drops its contents on the
table.

>   FIRST CLASSMATE
>   What IS that? They look like turds.
>   DEER turds.

LORRAINE picks up one of the three PRE-
SERVED PLUMS, eats it, then a second,
and licks her fingers.

>   LORRAINE
>   CHINESE deer turds.

>   SECOND CLASSMATE
>   That is SO disgusting, Rainey.

>   LORRAINE
>   (smug)
>   I know.

>   SECOND CLASSMATE
>   C'mon. Those weren't REALLY deer
>   turds. Were they?

>   FIRST CLASSMATE
>   Or tree bark.

> LORRAINE

Umm. Could be.

> SECOND CLASSMATE

Promise you'll bring even more disgusting Chinese desserts tomorrow? And eat them. Right in front of our eyes.

> LORRAINE

What will YOU bring if I say yes?

> SECOND CLASSMATE

My Mickey Mouse ears. Signed by Annette Funicello. I'll even let you try them on.

> LORRAINE
> (shaking hands with SECOND CLASSMATE)

It's a deal.

Second Classmate wipes her handshake hand with a paper napkin.

                                        CUT

It had been a couple of weeks since Denise forced Bert to hew to a schedule of maximum toilet training in a minimum of time and space. Especially after she returned home from school. Lorraine knew something was up because, after her sister attached the leash to Bert's collar, Denise always called out, too loudly:

"I'M HOME! I'M TAKING BERT OUT FOR A WALK NOW! A LONG WALK!"

Upon which Denise led Bert out the back door straight to Nai-nai's sandbox garden where he immediately defecated on one bok-choy plant, then peed on its closest neighbor.

"Bingo! Two birds with one turd. C'mon. That's long enough of a walk for you."

She tied him to the dogwood tree at the edge of the sandbox where he could lie in its shade and cool his stomach in the hole he'd dug while gnawing on the pacifying bone she'd given him. She climbed the big backyard hill, passed the ledge, entered the woods, passed their childhood hideouts and clubhouses to where civilization ended and where there was nothing but trees. When she was close enough to startle, Douglas stepped out from behind one of them. She never knew which one among so many, so she always was startled.

"Shhh," he whispered, wagging a pack of cigarettes in front of her eyes.

They found a tree suitable for climbing—there were already a chosen few but they liked to "go out on a limb" and look for yet another to add to their list of challenging but scalable specimens. They sat on separate branches not too far off the ground, smoking, rarely speaking between puffs. Denise flicked the butt of her finished cigarette away and began to climb higher.

"Hey, where do think you're going?"

"Where you can't follow me. You weigh more. The bough will break."

"And down will come baby, cradle and all," he sang.

She climbed higher. She wanted him to admire her agility, her daring. But what he wanted was for her to stop climbing. So he tried a different tune:

"I see England. I see France. I see Denny's underpants."

Which wasn't true, since she'd changed from her school clothes into blue jeans. He just wanted her to stop going any higher. She continued to climb. The branches supported her.

"That's high enough. Coming down is a lot harder—with more chance of a slip—than going up."

She smiled down at him and climbed higher.

"Denise!" he yelled, making nearby birds take flight.

Leo started making his way down from the top of the ladder Lorraine was holding steady against the front façade of the house. For the last hour, he'd been trimming branches from one of the sumac trees. When he reached the bottom rung, he set the saw down and wiped the sweat from his forehead with the back of his arm. He gazed at the littered ground, pleased with his handiwork, and lit up a cigarette. The shower he looked forward to was well-deserved and much-needed.

"Go find your sister. I want her to come shopping with me."

When Lorraine entered their bedroom, Denise was changing from her leaf-stained, sap-sticky clothes.

"Daddy's taking a shower. He wants you to go shopping with him," Lorraine said, flopping onto her bed.

Denise made a face, sat down at the vanity, and spritzed herself liberally with toilette water. "Again? You go."

"I went last time. To Yonkers. Remember? Where that Chinese man raises chickens in his garage." Lorraine rolled onto her back. "You reek…"

"Prince Matchabelli." Denise opened her mouth wide and gave the perfume bulb a firm squeeze.

"…of cigarettes," Lorraine concluded.

Denise whirled around, eyes narrowed, nostrils flared. "If you say anything…"

"I won't tell. Besides, Daddy won't even smell it. People who walk around in a cloud of cigarette smoke the way Daddy does can't smell a thing."

"What are you reading?" Leo asked in Mandarin, not taking his eyes off the almost empty road.

For emotional support and to make the shopping trip tolerable, Denise had taken André Gide along for the ride. *"The Return of the Prodigal Son,"* she answered, also in Mandarin, without looking up from the book. "By André Gide, a French writer."

"Your Chinese is improving," Leo said. "The accent. Even the tones."

Flattered, Denise glanced at him. "You really think so?" she continued in Mandarin. "My French teacher tells me I have a good ear for languages. *Douée,*" she said, in French, then reverted back to Mandarin. "Plus I've been listening to those Chinese tapes you bought us. A lot."

Leo took his right hand off the steering wheel and fumbled in his shirt pocket.

"Take the wheel, will you?" he said, in English.

Denise slid over closer to her father, who took a cigarette from the pack in his pocket and placed her left hand on the steering wheel.

"Both hands," he advised.

She slid closer to him and did as he said. Her left shoulder touched his right. "What do I do?" she asked, in English.

He lit the cigarette and rolled down the window. "Just hold it steady. There are no cars and the road is pretty straight for a while. Relax your grip."

For the next minute or so, Denise was, figuratively speaking, in the driver's seat. Leo guided the steering wheel as needed, which wasn't often, nor did it require more than a brief, bare touch of his left hand.

"So what's the book about? Keep your eyes on the road."

Denise was enjoying driving Katrinka, and she was pleased that her father was interested enough to ask.

"It's a short story. Based on the biblical story called *The Return of the Prodigal Son*. In a nutshell, a young man leaves his father's house, leads a very wicked life and returns home, broken and repentant."

"And his father takes him back?"

"Not only does he take him back, he throws a huge party for him. In fact, he loves his son even more now than he did before his son left home."

"That doesn't make sense."

"Well, that's how the biblical story goes. It's symbolic. It shows God's love for his children who've sinned against Him. In other words, all mankind. Everyone's guilty of original sin—guilty of being born human. But Gide's version is different. It starts where the biblical version ends: with the welcome home party."

Denise was on a roll. She felt like a pint-sized female Billy Graham.

"In Gide's version, and maybe the original version too—I've forgotten—the prodigal son has a younger brother. He wants to know all about his older brother's life after he left their father's house and went out into the world. The prodigal son tells him all the wicked, terrible things he did and saw. He leaves out nothing. Guess what the younger brother does, now that he knows what kind of life his brother led?"

"He kills him."

"Uh-uh. He asks for his brother's blessing. Just like the prodigal son asked for his father's forgiveness when he returned home. Because now that he knows what his brother went through, he knows that he must leave home too. And he needs his brother's blessing to do that."

"Why not his *father's* blessing? Why his brother's?" Leo said, a small "v" incising itself between his brows. "The father didn't sin. The father led a good life. He forgave, didn't he? It was the son who brought shame on the family."

"Because it was the son who had *suffered*," Denise answered. "It was the son who had *lived*."

"It still doesn't make sense."

"Yeah. I guess so." She took a deep breath. "Daddy, who's Natasha?"

"What are you talking about? You're gripping the steering wheel again."

"When we used to go to Grampa's for our Mandarin lessons, he'd be in the next room reading his newspapers. Sometimes he'd fall asleep and he'd say, 'Natasha' over and over again in his sleep."

Leo frowned and shook his head. "Natasha. I don't know any Natasha."

"Once we asked Aiying who Natasha is. She said she sometimes heard Grampa saying Natasha when he was dozing in his chair and even when he was awake. She said she didn't know who Natasha is. But she did say that Grampa sometimes said other things too. Along with Natasha."

"Like?"

"Like about you." When her father didn't say anything, she continued, "Grampa would say, 'Oh, my son. My beloved, my lost, son.'"

Leo grabbed the wheel. "That's enough. I'll steer now."

Denise slid over in the passenger seat until her right shoulder touched the car door.

EXT. LIN HOUSE - DAY

A chauffeur-driven limousine pulls up
in front of the house. Guoxin gets out.
He's wearing an impeccable three-piece
suit and an expensive fedora and carries
a large suitcase. We follow him up the
driveway and along the flagstone path to
the backyard sandbox garden where Nai-nai
is tending her vegetables. He sets the
suitcase down at the edge of the sandbox,
doffs his fedora. Nai-nai sees him and
stops hoeing. All dialogue is in Mandarin.

> NAI-NAI
>
> *Ni hao.* (notices the suitcase) Are
> you running away from home?

> GUOXIN
>
> You could say that. Evelyn is in
> New Jersey playing mah-jongg with
> her friends.

> NAI-NAI
>
> Leo's not here. He went shopping
> with Denise.

> GUOXIN
>
> I didn't come to see Leo.

> NAI-NAI
>
> Have you eaten? I haven't started
> making dinner yet, but I could make
> you…

                    GUOXIN
Thank you, I'm not hungry. I've
come to see you.

                    NAI-NAI
(pause) It's been a long time.

                    GUOXIN
Have I changed that much?

                    NAI-NAI
        (fussing with her hair bun)
I have.

                    GUOXIN
No.

                    NAI-NAI
YOU haven't changed. Always the
diplomat!

                    GUOXIN
        (looking around at her garden)
And you've inherited your father's
green thumb.

                    NAI-NAI
        (smiling, pleased)
When I saw what my granddaughters…
OUR granddaughters… were eating
(shudders)… Are you sure you wouldn't
like a little soup? Gow-gay, your favorite. (pause) That is, it used to
be your favorite. A long time ago.

                         GUOXIN
                    (shakes his head)

Take me on a tour of your gardens,
will you? I'd like that.

Guoxin and Nai-nai stroll along the
footpaths between rows of vegetables.
We see them from behind — silhouetted
by the setting sun. Nai-nai points to
or touches her plants tenderly. Guoxin
walks close behind her. From the back,
they could be lovers, or an old married
couple.

                         GUOXIN
You've made a good life for yourself here in America. Surrounded by
your gardens, and your family.

                         NAI-NAI
There are times when I'm lonely.

                         GUOXIN
I'm lonely most of the time.

                         NAI-NAI
(pause) Now that Leo has sold the
factory, he spends time at home
with me. But Margaret works. The
girls go to school. Their Chinese is improving, so I shouldn't
complain.

                    GUOXIN

Living in America is like being under house arrest. In Shanghai, family and friends filled my house all
hours of the day and night. Here,
I have few friends. My home has no
renao. It lacks the warmth of close
human relationships — like yours.

                    NAI-NAI

Here everyone works. No one has
time. Even the closest of relatives
see each other just a few times a
year. And guests in America have it
really tough. Just because you're
invited to come by, it doesn't mean
you're invited to share a meal together. And when you are — imagine!
— you have to bring your own food!
They call that pot luck. I call it
bad luck.

                    GUOXIN

That's nothing. Here when the children grow up and their "old man"
stops working, they leave home.
They seldom return to visit. They
don't take care of their parents in
their old age.

NAI-NAI

We're fortunate, aren't we, that
Leo isn't selfish like that.

GUOXIN

No, HE isn't. But I am.

NAI-NAI

That's not so.

GUOXIN

Even if you don't think so, he does.
And I have to agree. I haven't been
a good husband. I haven't taken
care of you — both before and after
Evelyn.

NAI-NAI

You're being too hard on yourself.

GUOXIN

I wanted Leo to fill my shoes, professionally. Instead, he's succeeded where I've failed — personally.
You're my primary wife. I haven't
taken care of you as I should.

NAI-NAI

That's the past. The past is over.
This is now. And it's the first time
I'm seeing you in ten years.

                    GUOXIN

We can thank whoever invented mah-
jongg for that.

They both smile warmly at each other.

                    GUOXIN
                  (solemnly)

I don't feel the way you do — that
the past is over. Not when I've
failed to fulfill my obligations to
you.

Nai-nai turns away from him to hide the
feelings he's stirred in her. She picks
vegetables and puts them in a basket all
the while that she speaks.

                    NAI-NAI

If you can't forget the past, then
you must choose what part of the
past you want to remember. I remember, for example, my father and
yours, how close they were, despite
the great difference in their back-
grounds. Your father, a Mandarin.
My father, his gardener. When you
were a child, you practiced calligraphy with your tutor. And I hid
behind the plum tree my father had
planted in your garden, watching.
You hated grinding the ink stick
to make the ink just the right

blackness and consistency.You just
wanted to write — character after
character, poem after poem. (wags
her head) Who would have thought
that one day we would marry! It
caused quite a stir — even a scandal of sorts.

Nai-nai turns around. Guoxin is gone.
C.U. of the SUITCASE he's left behind.

LIN HOUSE - DAY

We hear Chinese-style music performed on
the traditional instruments of *pipa* and
erhu which play throughout this scene.

Leo holds Lorraine's tap shoes in front
of her mortified face, then drops them
into the wastepaper basket. He leads her
outside to the front lawn and shows her
the first few steps of 24-step tai qi.
His movements are smooth and graceful.
When he repeats them and gestures her to
follow along with him, Lorraine is stiff
and clumsy.

In the background, we see that the sumac
tree branches are a bit shorter as well
as shorn of almost all their twigs.

LIN HOUSE - LATER THE SAME DAY

> Leo marches into the dining room where
> Denise is doing her homework and word-
> lessly sweeps her school books off to one
> side. In their place, he sets a book of
> Chinese calligraphy, sheets of rice pa-
> per, a bottle of ink, and a few callig-
> raphy brushes of different sizes. He ex-
> ecutes some simple ideograms. They are
> beautiful. He hands the brush to Denise.
> She tries to follow his example. Her
> ideograms look like Rorschach blots.

LIN HOUSE - DAY — A FEW DAYS LATER

> On the front lawn, Leo and Lorraine
> practice tai qi together, side by side.
> She has improved. Her movements are more
> fluid, calmer.

> The sumac branches are shorter still.

LIN HOUSE - LATER THE SAME DAY

Seated at the dining room table, Denise
practices writing Chinese characters. Leo
stands beside her, looking on, guiding the
brush only when she needs help. Her ideograms are much improved, and the way she
holds the brush is correct: on the vertical,
firmly but without gripping. She looks up at
him for confirmation. He nods his head.

LIN HOUSE - DAY — A FEW DAYS LATER

Lorraine performs the entire 24-step tai
qi sequence without misstep while Leo
watches. When she finishes, they both
smile.

The sumac branches are even shorter.
Some are no more than stumps.

LIN HOUSE - LATER THE SAME DAY

Leo and Denise sit across from each other at the dining room table. Denise sets
down her calligraphy brush and assess-
es the ideograms of the poem she has
just copied. The Chinese music played
throughout this scene stops.

                    LEO
        First, in English.

                  DENISE
            (reciting by heart)

Drinking Alone with the Moon by Li
Po. (clears her throat) From a pot
of wine among the flowers/I drank
alone. There was no one with me —/
Till raising my cup, I asked the
bright moon/To bring me my shadow
and make us three.

                    LEO
        Now in Chinese.

Denise recites the poem in Mandarin by
heart, pausing only once, then continues
seamlessly on to the end, when she beams
with accomplishment.

                                        CUT

Saturday afternoon. The housework and yard work accomplished, Margaret went to get a manicure and a pedicure. Or so she'd said. Leo decided to use the opportunity (or the ruse) to find out what all the fuss was about. After all, Margaret wasn't the only person to possess a hidden agenda.

He drove Katrinka to St. Agatha's Church. Though he'd taken his family there every Sunday for years, this was the first time he entered the church. *Their* sanctuary. He was invading *their* place of worship. Though it took his eyes several seconds to get used to the darkness, his sense of smell was immediately assaulted by beeswax candles burning, flowers wilting, the musky residue of days-old incense. The rose window at the far end of the nave came into focus, a kaleidoscope of deep reds, blues, and yellows. As his eyes adjusted, monstrous figures loomed out of the shadows, all of them with sad, desolate expressions on their faces. One of them wore a crown of thorns. Blood dripped down his gaunt, agonized face. And why wouldn't he be agonized? The wretched man was nailed to a cross by his hands and feet. Leo had walked into a torture chamber. Here was proof that Western methods surpassed, or at least rivaled, the Chinese inventions of water torture and forcing sharp needles under the victim's fingernails.

The depiction of all the suffering and mortification around him were both offset and exaggerated by what Leo saw when he looked up. Painted on the ceiling, obese pink infants flew around on stunted wings much too stubby for their corpulent bodies to even obtain lift-off let alone remain airborne. They flitted around a man with long hair who had pulled opened his chest to expose a heart that was not only on fire but also emitting what looked like lethal gold daggers. Head and arms upraised, mouth slightly ajar, a nearby woman swooned in anguish. Or in ecstasy. It was difficult to tell which. On both sides of the center aisle of the nave, several people—mostly young—sat in the wooden pews, hands clasped, heads bowed. Despite such solemn poses, they appeared to be much happier than the representations of the holy folks surrounding them. The girls wore white doilies—like the kind that went under cakes—on their heads fastened to their hair by Bobby pins. One of the girls had opted for a Kleenex instead. An odd choice for a head covering, Leo thought. Then again, both were.

Eschewing the intimidating center aisle, Leo walked down a side aisle where he peered at a plaque on the wall that described the "Fourteen Stations of the Cross." Before he could finish reading it, the back door of the church opened admitting an intense blast of daylight that outlined his two daughters in silhouette. Leo froze in place. Luckily, Denise and Lorraine were so busy whispering to each other as they entered the vestibule that they failed to notice him. Nor were they able to see clearly until their eyes adjusted to the gloom—time enough for Leo to escape undetected into a suffocatingly tiny booth behind a heavy maroon velvet curtain a few feet away. What luck!

"It's all Daddy's fault that I had to tell Sister Patrick that Pluto's going to college in California," Lorraine lamented, "and that's why she doesn't come home often. Now I've got one more venial sin to confess. Two."

"Sister Patrick didn't ask about me?"

"At least I didn't have to lie about *you*. I told her you weren't anywhere near first in your class at Bronx Science since Jewish kids are a lot smarter than Catholics."

Denise retaliated by pushing her sister into the nave. "Let's go to Monsignor Riordan. He's got no one waiting outside his confessional. And he gives light sentences, uh, penances."

As luck would have it, the booth in which Leo had taken refuge was part of Monsignor Riordan's confessional box. He heard a slight rasping noise. The sound of the confessional window slowly sliding back, exposing a thick screen.

"Wha..? Who's there?" Leo said. He peered through the screen but saw only a murky shadow on the other side of it.

"Monsignor Riordan, your confessor," came a low whisper. "And you don't have to tell me who you are. I already know."

"How can you know that?" Leo hissed, breaking out in a cold sweat and retracting his head away from the window.

"You're a child of God who wants me, His representative on earth, to hear your confession. You may begin."

"Begin?"

"Has it been *that* long since you've been to confession?"

"I've never made a confession in my life."

"Ah, a recent convert!"

Leo drew back the heavy curtain an inch and peeked out. He saw the backs of Denise and Lorraine seated in the pew directly in front of him.

"That's nothing to be ashamed of, my son. You should be proud to be making your first confession as an adult. I'm here to listen. To help."

The woman occupying the booth on the other side of the confessional exited and Denise entered in her place.

"Confession begins by saying,'Bless me, Father, for I have sinned.

It has been…' and you state how long it's been since your last confession. But since this is your first confession, you may say that."

Leo ducked his head back inside the booth.

"All right. This is my first confession."

"Now you may tell me your sins."

"Actually, since this is my first time, I'm a bit nervous. Would
you mind listening to the confession of the person in the other
booth first? While I get my sins in order."

"If a bit more time will make you feel more at ease," Monsignor
Riordan conceded before sliding the window shut.

Leo heard the window on the other side of the confessional
sliding open, Denise's muffled and therefore incomprehensible
admission and enumeration of wrongdoing. He peeked outside the
booth. Lorraine was awaiting her turn to unburden herself of her
sins. She gazed at the statues of the Virgin Mary and Child, St.
Joseph, Christ crucified, at the ceiling with its the paintings of the
risen Christ, the cherubim and seraphim. When Denise exited the
confessional and headed for the altar rail to say her penance, Lorraine disappeared into the vacated booth, allowing Leo a perfectly
timed and executed getaway.

Monsignor Riordan slid open Leo's window.

"I'm ready to hear your confession, my son. My son?"

That night, while Margaret lay asleep, her finger- and toenails
varnished in *Cherries in the Snow*, Leo sat at his desk piled high
with tabloid newspapers and gossip magazines bought at Freddie's
Corner (soda *jerk*—fitting appellation—be damned). From these
tawdry publications, he cut out articles which when numerous
enough would constitute part of an ingenious plan, a form of psychological warfare he believed would result in certain victory. He'd
told his wife that he wouldn't be needing the car the following day,

that she could drive Katrinka to church and bring home the Sunday papers and baked goods afterwards. He had other plans.

7:30 a.m. Sunday morning. Leo was still sleeping. Margaret got out of bed and walked into the en suite bathroom. On the sink, in the water glass that held her toothbrush, there was a newspaper article. She extracted it and read: *Indian widow commits suttee in Queens apartment after death of husband of 45 years.* She looked over her shoulder at Leo, then flushed it down the toilet.

8:00 a.m. Dressed for Mass, Margaret woke her daughters. In the kitchen, she opened the can of coffee in the refrigerator and pulled out a magazine article. The headline read: *Divorced socialite foiled in second suicide attempt.* After she tossed it in the garbage can, she heard the whine of the front door opening, then clicking shut, followed soon afterwards by the rasping of a dull-bladed handsaw gnawing into wood. To her ears it sounded like the grunting and groaning of excruciatingly mismatched lovers.

8:30 a.m. The sound of sawing continued, then stopped, replaced by Leo's voice warning Nai-nai who, Margaret assumed, was holding the ladder, to move away. The shout "TIMBER" followed, then the thud of something large and heavy—presumably a sumac branch—hitting the ground. A Tarzan-ish yodel, so out of Leo's character, rent the still morning air, startling Margaret. *What next?* she thought. *His two fists thumping his breastbone like a kettledrum and the sight of him swinging past the kitchen window on a vine from the stinkweed tree?* She opened a box of cereal. Along with the corn flakes, out came a newspaper article whose headline read: *"Lonely divorcée found axe-murdered in squalid cold-water flat."* Margaret ripped it up and threw it in the garbage can.

School's out. Finally. No more homework, no more books, no more teachers' dirty looks, as the saying goes. Instead, while their classmates go off to their country cottages or vacation somewhere exciting, Denise and Lorraine are imprisoned at home where there's plenty of house- and yard work for them to do, Chinese language lessons for them to learn, and calligraphy for Denise and tai qi for Lorraine to continue to practice.

Unlike school, gow-gay season isn't over. Thankfully, though, it's coming to an end. Today it's Denise's turn to take Nai-nai to the medians along Cranston Road where the wild greens grow. Under towering horse chestnut trees that shelter the allée of gow-gay bushes, Nai-nai starts filling a brown paper grocery bag with what Denise hopes is the last of the tender leaves. A Cadillac passes by slowly. When the silver-maned driver peers out the window and gives Nai-nai a disdainful once-over, Denise's head sinks into her shoulders. Her heart sinks even lower in shame.

Just then, rounding the corner and heading their way, Douglas pops into view. Denise's heart rises instantaneously to her throat, where it pounds in terror. She scurries across the street to conceal herself behind a privet hedge (too late) and to pretend that Nai-nai isn't hers (so far, so good, since her grandmother is foraging on the far side of the slightly quivering gow-gay bush and therefore invisible from both her and Douglas's vantage points).

"Hi," Douglas says, approaching.

"Hi," Denise answers, feigning admiration for the privet hedge.

"Fancy meeting you here."

"Yes. Fancy."

Keeping her head stock still, she rolls her eyes in Nai-nai's direction. She releases a tremulous sigh. The culprit is still hidden by the gow-gay bush.

"Doing anything special right now?"

"Uh, no," Denise says offhandedly.

"Got time for…"

He looks around guardedly—no pedestrians, no cars, doesn't notice the gow-gay bush suffering from St. Vitus dance—and pulls out a pack of cigarettes from his jeans pocket.

"Sure. Maybe just one."

"C'mon," Douglas says and takes her hand.

She resists.

"Where are we going?"

"Well, we can't smoke here, can we?"

"Somewhere close by, then."

"The woods in back of your house."

"Not my house. It's too far."

"Three blocks?"

"The field at Sutcliffe Country Day," Denise says, pointing in the direction away from Nai-nai and the gow-gay bush. "Behind the honeysuckle bushes growing along the fence." She extricates her hand and begins to run. "Come on!"

"Hey, what's the rush?" he shouts, and takes off after her.

Nai-nai steps out from behind the gow-gay bush and watches Denise and Douglas running off. A long black car—the same one that drove by a few minutes ago—drives by again, this time from the opposite direction, this time even more slowly. Nai-nai looks at the man in the driver's seat with mild curiosity. He looks back at her with undisguised suspicion.

INT. LAO CAO'S OFFICE - DAY

Lao Cao sits behind his desk, reading a document. Leo bursts into his office, throws *The Wall Street Journal* down on his desk. The conversation is in Mandarin.

> LEO
> (irate)

Explain this.

Lao Cao glances at the newspaper.

> LAO CAO
> (calmly)

You seem angry. You should be pleased.

> LEO
> (struggling to control himself)

Pleased that you stabbed me in the back? You, my stockbroker. More than that — my college roommate. (bitterly) My friend.

> LAO CAO

As your stockbroker — AND your friend — I bought you shares in a company that I thought would make you some money. I was wrong. It will make you a LOT of money. It already has.

                    LEO
You bought me shares in the compa-
ny of my RIVAL, my ARCH ENEMY, my
NEMESIS! He stabbed me in the back
when he was my manager — and now
YOU'VE twisted it. You BETRAYED me!

                  LAO CAO
How have I betrayed you?

                    LEO
You put my money into the company
of the man who ruined me. Who stole
my factory out from under me. Who…

English is spoken from here on in.

                  LAO CAO
…bought your factory at a fair price
and who changed it from a dinosaur
into a dynamo. He saw that the era
of condensers is over. Tomorrow,
computer chips will be king. He had
foresight. He had vision. He bet on
the future, and he won.

                    LEO
              (disconsolate)
And I lost. I lost.

EXT. THE FIELD AT SUTCLIFFE COUNTRY DAY
SCHOOL

Douglas and Denise are smoking cigarettes. They are hidden behind some honeysuckle bushes growing along the chain
link fence. Denise takes one of the
blossoms and gingerly extracts the pis-
til so that the droplet of honeysuckle
nectar remains suspended on the end of
it. She tilts back her head, opens her
mouth, and touches the droplet with the
tip of her tongue.

                    DOUGLAS
          How about just one more?

                    DENISE
               (shaking her head)
          I'd better…

                    DOUGLAS
          How about one cigarette's pleasure
          doubled, then? I'll show you how.

Douglas lights up and drags on a cigarette. He gestures for her to open her
mouth, then he blows smoke into it. When
Denise begins coughing, they both burst
out laughing.

INT. LAO CAO'S OFFICE

                    LAO CAO
No, Lao Lin. You WON. He won. And
you won. Maris Electric Company is
now Eddington Electronics. You own
one thousand shares of Eddington
Trading Corporation. Do you know
what that means? I bought you one
thousand shares the minute Eddington went public. Since then, your
shares have split twice. TWICE.
That's how much their value has
risen. You now own four thousand
shares of Eddington Trading Corporation. (he smiles) Enough to have
a voice on their board.

                    LEO
          (collapsing into a chair)
I have no interest in being a member of their board. Of any board.
I have no interest in business. Of
any kind. (rakes his fingers through
his hair) I never did. I have no
interest in anything anymore.

                    LAO CAO
          (softer tone of voice)
In college you were quite the poet.

Leo scoffs.

                    LAO CAO

No, you were good. Good enough to
impress the girls, as I recall.
Margaret especially. And a number
of professors. Have you kept at it?

                    LEO
              (sarcastically)

One poet in the family is enough,
don't you think?

                    LAO CAO

A shame. But you're right. Professor Huang — remember Professor
Huang? — he wanted you to publish
some of your haiku. Even found a
publisher who was interested.

                    LEO

A publisher who wanted me to trans-
late my father's poetry into English, accompanied by some of my
poems. (recalls) Each haiku of mine
was a response to one of my father's poems. (sardonically) Two
for the price of one.

                    LAO CAO

Yes, to add depth, a new level of
meaning to your father's poems and
paintings. (steeples his fingers)
Together with a preface — an essay,
written by you — it would make an

exceptional book.

                    LEO
Might have.

                    LAO CAO
Would. WILL.

                    LEO
I'm not a poet. I'm not a writer.

                    LAO CAO
You wanted to be. Before the civil war. And then the revolution
changed everything. For me as well.
(smiles sadly) But we came through
it, didn't we? We came to America.

EXT. CRANSTON ROAD

Denise is running down the street. She
stops at the gow-gay bush. Nai-nai is
gone.

                    DENISE
              (looks around frantically;
              calls)
Nai-nai! NAI-NAI!

INT. LIN HOUSE

Denise, breathless, runs into the living room. Lorraine is practicing tai qi
while watching TV. C.U. of TV screen: a

news program shows children performing
Mao's LOYALTY DANCE and waving his LIT-
TLE RED BOOK.

> DENISE
> (anxiously)
>
> Have you seen Nai-nai?

> LORRAINE
> (without stopping her tai qi)
>
> I thought she was with you.

INT. NAI-NAI'S ROOM.

Denise bursts into Nai-nai's room without knocking. No Nai-nai.

INT. MASTER BEDROOM

Denise bursts into the master bedroom
without knocking. Leo sits on his side
of the bed, telephone receiver to his
ear.

> LEO
> (into receiver)
>
> I'll be right there. (hangs up) You.
> Come with me.

INT. KATRINKA

Leo drives, cigarette in hand. Denise
sits slouched in the passenger seat.

EXT. POLICE STATION

> Leo drives up to the station and parks
> outside the entrance. He and Denise exit
> Katrinka and enter the building.

INT. JAIL CELL

> C.U. of Nai-nai behind bars.

>> OFFICER (O.S.)
> Your mother was picked up for tres-
> passing. We got a call from a res-
> ident of Cranston Road. He said
> he'd spotted a suspicious-looking
> character…

>> LEO (C.U.)
> You mean, someone who looks foreign.

>> OFFICER
> Mr. Lin, I'm just repeating what he
> told one of my men. Soon after that,
> we got another phone call, also
> from a Cranston Road resident, say-
> ing that there was, and I quote, "a
> strange woman hanging by her arms
> from the magnolia tree in my front
> yard." We knew when we saw her —
> unfortunately, we couldn't communi-
> cate with her — that there was some
> mistake. She was obviously lost.

C.U. of Nai-nai's face.

                    OFFICER
        Not a vagrant. Not a loiterer. Not
        a trespasser in the usual sense of
        the word.

C.U. of jangling KEYS, KEY turning in
lock; jail DOOR opening.

                    OFFICER
        I'm sorry for the error, and the
        inconvenience…

                    LEO
        To say nothing of the shame brought
        upon me and my family.

                    OFFICER
                 (exhales)
        Your mother is free to go.

INT. KATRINKA

Leo drives, puffing furiously on a cigarette. Nai-nai sits in the front passenger seat. Denise slouches in the back
seat.

                    NAI-NAI
            (to LEO, in Mandarin)
        And the next thing I knew, Denise
        wasn't there. So I just continued
        picking gow-gay.

                    LEO
          (to DENISE, in English)
Where did you go when you left
Nai-nai?

                  DENISE
              (sullenly)
Sutcliffe Country Day School.

                  NAI-NAI
There was this strange-looking man
who passed me in a car the size of
a small airplane. He drove by a few
times. After a while I felt tired.
I knew that hanging from a tree
branch would make me feel better. I
didn't think anyone would mind. I
don't weigh very much.

                    LEO
              (to DENISE)
With whom?

                  DENISE
A friend. From school.

                  NAI-NAI
Then these two very nice gentlemen
came and escorted me to their car.
I thought it was some kind of play-
thing — with its whirling lights
and all.

                    LEO
                (to DENISE)
    Why?

                    DENISE
    To smoke. Cigarettes he'd brought
    along.

                    NAI-NAI
    They were very friendly. They even
    had me sit between them. I'm sure
    Denise didn't mean to be away so
    long. She just lost track of the
    time.

                    LEO
                (to DENISE)
    How many? How many did you smoke?

                    DENISE
    One. No. Two. And a half. Dunhills.

INT. LIN MASTER BEDROOM

    Leo stands in front of DENISE, an unopened
    pack of Kent cigarettes in his hand.

                    LEO
    Since you like to smoke so much,
    here. (hands her the pack) You're
    going to stay here until you fin-
    ish every cigarette in that pack.
    You're going to show me twenty cig-
    arette butts.

Leo exits the bathroom, slamming the
door behind him. Denise scowls, lights
up a cigarette and puffs insouciantly. As
smoke starts filling the bathroom, she
opens the window, sticks her head out
and sees a car pull up. A car she's never seen before. A STATION WAGON. To her
surprise, Margaret exits from the front
passenger seat.

                                         CUT

Should he ask, she'd tell him that she was wearing a new brand of perfume. One with notes of gardenia. Or rose. Or jasmine. Or a combination of all three. Not a fragrance, of course, that she had on her dressing table, that he'd smelled before. This one she'd sampled today, at the perfume counter at Saks. Should he ask. Hopefully, he wouldn't. Wouldn't even notice the scent at all. She checked her clothes. From the bottom of one of her shoes, she peeled off a leaf, then scraped both soles free of dirt as she walked up the driveway. What luck that Leo hadn't been home to take her call and pick her up at the subway station! It had given them more precious time to be together in the station wagon. She'd say she took a cab. If he asked. So as not to bother him. She took a deep breath and opened the front door. Lorraine was in front of the TV practicing tai qi. It was a form Margaret didn't recognize.

"Hi, Rainey. Daddy home? Oh, he'll be so happy to see how much progress you've made."

"Upstairs," Lorraine said, her eyes not budging from the television screen. She was intent on watching those Chinese children perform a dance in honor of Chairman Mao. She gritted her teeth. She vowed she'd learn the steps by heart if it was the last thing she ever did.

When Margaret entered the bedroom, Leo was sitting at his desk reading the newspaper. Fresh cigarette smoke stung her eyes and nostrils despite the fact that Leo wasn't smoking.

"Don't go in the bathroom. If you have to, use the girls' bathroom."

Margaret stopped taking off her bolero, its armholes at her elbows, like a straitjacket. "Why?"

Leo looked at Margaret accusingly.

"Denise *abandoned* Nai-nai and went off with one of her juvenile delinquent friends. To smoke cigarettes."

Margaret glanced at the closed bathroom door. The cigarette smoke. Now it made sense. But she didn't want it to. "Where's Nai-nai? Is she all right?"

"I found her at the police station. She'd been arrested for vagrancy," He stood up and walked towards Margaret. "The wife of Lin Guoxin—arrested! All because of your delinquent daughter."

"Leo…"

"I had to beg the police officer not to press charges. Can you imagine? *My mother*—with a criminal record."

"And Denise?"

Margaret's arms—her entire body—slackened, allowing her bolero to slide to the floor. Leo crossed his arms over his chest.

"She's getting what's coming to her."

INT. MASTER BATHROOM

Denise finishes the cigarette, stubs
it out, and sets it on the rim of the
bathtub.

                    DENISE
          One down. Nineteen to go.

She lights up another cigarette, puffs on
it, looks at it, and makes a disgusted
face.

                    DENISE
          Give me Dunhills any day.

Her eyes light up with a brilliant idea.
She sets the second lit cigarette on the
bathtub rim, then a third, until she has
a dozen lit cigarettes going, all set in
a row on the bathtub rim. She opens the
window wide and stares out of it while
smoking a cigarette and reciting verses
from Baudelaire's *Les Fleurs du Mal* in
French interspersed with verses from the
Tang Dynasty poet Li Po in Mandarin.

The breeze enters the bathroom through
the window ruffling and billowing the
shower curtain, which grazes some of the
lit cigarettes. Lost in reverie, Denise
doesn't see that the curtain behind her
has started to smoke, then catches fire.

173

The acrid smell of the burning shower
curtain causes Denise to turn her head
and see that a quarter of the curtain is
in flames. Petrified, she presses herself
up against the rear wall near the open
window. Now a third of the curtain is
ablaze and starting to detach from the
curtain rod, preventing her from getting
to the door. She takes a bath towel but,
in trying to put out the fire with it,
she only fans the flames higher. Half the
curtain is now on fire, cutting off her
escape route. She coughs, puts the bath
towel against her nose and mouth.

                                      CUT

"Where is she?" Margaret asked.

Instinctively she moved towards the bathroom, but Leo barred the way and stood in front of the door.

"Inside. She likes to smoke? Let her smoke a whole pack."

"That's not a punishment," Margaret said, livid, her hands clenched into fists. "That's...

"DADDY! Open the door!"

"Not until you've finished every last one."

"Leo, if you don't..." Margaret began. She stared at the dark gray smoke—smoke not the color of tobacco smoke—seeping into the bedroom from under the bathroom door. It was a sight that cut off her words in a single stroke, that made her mute. The acrid smell—a smell she knew wasn't tobacco smoke—paralyzed her, filled her with dread.

"DADDY! PLEASE!"

Margaret lunged towards the door, knocking Leo against it.

"DADDY! The shower curtain's on fire! DADDY!"

In his mind's eye, Leo saw a raging wall of fire. It was a sight that blinded him to Margaret's horror-stricken face and the blackish smoke creeping into their bedroom, pinched his nostrils closed against the stench of burning plastic, shut his ears to Denise's anguished cries. Leo heard only a single desperate word.

"BABA! BABA!"

Margaret's full, struggling weight pressed Leo up against the bathroom door. The heat he felt singed his back, inflamed his mind. With the power that terror conferred on him, he shoved her away from him with the physical strength of a man twice his size.

"VLADIMIR! VLADIMIR!" Leo screamed.

He yanked open the door. One arm flung across his face, he grabbed a bath towel with the other and pulled the half-destroyed curtain off the rod. After smothering it with the towel and stomping out the remaining flames with his feet, he led Denise out of the bathroom.

"Are you all right? Are you hurt?" he yelled into her face, shaking her by the shoulders.

Denise tried to stifle the urge to cry, unsuccessfully. Her mouth contorted and wobbled open, emitting hiccuping, choking sounds.

"You scared the living daylights out of me! Do you know that? You scared the living daylights out of me."

Leo gently cupped her tear-streaked, runny-nosed face in his hands. The gesture stopped the crying cold. Denise looked at her father as though he was unrecognizable. Rather, she recognized that she knew nothing about this man who was her father, this stranger. Remembering himself, Leo let his arms fall to his sides and pulled back from her.

Margaret opened the bedroom windows wide and turned on the standing fan to clear the air of smoke. She crossed the threshold into the bathroom and looked around dispassionately.

"Vladimir," she said, turning to face Leo.

"What?" The word confused and disoriented him.

"That's what you shouted. Twice. Vladimir."

Leo turned and looked at Denise with an expression that both entreated and commanded her to be complicit, to contradict what

Margaret had just said, to validate what he was about to say. "No, I didn't."

"Who's Vladimir?" Denise asked, her need to know greater than any fear of retribution or punishment.

Leo's pupils contracted. His voice became thin, hard, brittle. Whatever momentary display of affection he'd just shown her vanished, never happened.

"Go to your room. You'll finish memorizing Li Po's 'Drinking Alone with the Moon.' You'll come back here in one-half hour and recite it to me. Word for word. One-half hour. No mistakes." By a slight tilt of his chin towards the door, Leo signaled that she had his permission to withdraw. "One last thing," he added, stopping Denise mid-step. "You'll eat the gow-gay soup Nai-nai's making for dinner. Every last leaf."

The smoke had cleared, but the smell of the cigarettes and burnt plastic hung heavy in the air. Heavier for Leo, however, was the weight of Margaret's eyes boring into him. She was incensed by the harsh punishment he'd meted out to their daughter, mortified by its life-threatening result, grateful for his heroic rescue of her, stunned by his utterance of a name she'd never heard before, but even more by the depth of emotion behind it, saddened by his brusque dismissal of Denise after a brief but tender show of affection.

"I'll clean up the bathroom."

He could tell by the throaty rasp of her voice that she was exhausted emotionally by the cascade of chaotic feelings set in motion by an irresponsible decision on Denise's part that led to an excessive penalty on his own and the terrifying outcome that no one could have predicted.

"No, I'll do it," he told her.

"It's just the shower curtain that's destroyed," she said. "No real damage done."

"No. No real damage done."

EXT. SAKS FIFTH AVENUE'S WINDOW DISPLAY -
A FEW DAYS LATER

Wearing dark glasses and a fedora, Leo
conceals himself behind a lamppost on
the southeast corner of St. Patrick's
Cathedral. He's spying on Margaret who
is standing on a ladder in a window display of Saks while she dresses a manne-
quin in a black velvet gown. She is as-
sisted by a WINDOW DRESSER — male, young,
handsome. As she descends the ladder, he
takes her by the waist to steady her.

They are talking animatedly. We see them
but we can't hear them because they are
behind the glass window. Instead, we
share Leo's P.O.V out on the street.

C.U. of Leo who, in his jealousy, puts
the words he both fears and imagines
them to be saying in their mouths.

                    MARGARET
             (mouthing the words, but in
             LEO's voice)
        It's so much fun working with you.
        I don't know when I've felt this
        young in ages.

INT. SAKS' WINDOW DISPLAY

                    MARGARET
          (what she *really* is saying to
          WINDOW DRESSER)

     I think the mannequin's hand should
     be palm down, not up. What do you
     think?

EXT. SAKS' WINDOW DISPLAY

                    WINDOW DRESSER
          (mouthing the words, in LEO's
          voice)

     You're the most beautiful woman
     I've ever met. (kisses mannequin's
     hand) I think I'm falling in love
     with you.

INT. SAKS' WINDOW DISPLAY

                    WINDOW DRESSER
          (what he is *really* saying to
          MARGARET)

     I think you're right. (turns the
     mannequin's hand palm side down,
     kisses the top of its hand) It's
     more elegant. It shows off the
     bracelet to better advantage too.

EXT. SAKS' WINDOW DISPLAY

                    MARGARET
          (mouthing the words, in LEO's
          voice)

Don't ever let my husband hear
you say that!

INT. SAKS' WINDOW DISPLAY

                    MARGARET
         (what she is *really* saying to
         WINDOW DRESSER)

     That way the clasp is out of sight,
     where it belongs.

EXT. SAKS' WINDOW DISPLAY

                WINDOW DRESSER
         (mouthing the words, in LEO's
         voice)

     When can we see each other in pri-
     vate? (looks around the window)
     I'm tired of meeting you in this
     fishbowl.

INT. SAKS' WINDOW DISPLAY

                WINDOW DRESSER
         (what he is *really* saying to
         MARGARET)

     What do you think about the idea
     of (looks at the window) painting
     a frame around the window?

EXT. SAKS' WINDOW DISPLAY

                    MARGARET
          (mouthing the words, in LEO'S
          voice)

     I don't know… (fingers her lower lip)
     It would be difficult.

INT. SAKS' WINDOW DISPLAY

                    MARGARET
          (what she is *really* saying to
          WINDOW DRESSER)

     Hmmm. (fingers her lower lip) You
     mean, to emphasize the portrait
     quality of the gown.

EXT. SAKS' WINDOW DISPLAY

                 WINDOW DRESSER
          (mouthing the words, in LEO's
          voice)

     After closing. My place. Just tell
     your husband you have to work late.

INT. SAKS' WINDOW DISPLAY

                 WINDOW DRESSER
          (what he is *really* saying to
          MARGARET)

     Exactly. Like a painting by John
     Singer Sargent.

EXT. SAKS' WINDOW DISPLAY

>   MARGARET
>   (mouthing the words, in LEO's
>   voice)
>   Okay — I'll do it!

INT. SAKS' WINDOW DISPLAY

>   MARGARET
>   (what she is *really* saying to
>   WINDOW DRESSER)
>   Good idea — let's add it.

Window Dresser and Margaret fold the
ladder and exit Window Display. Seething,
Leo steps out from behind the lamppost
and hurries away, but not before taking
a long look at ST. PATRICK'S CATHEDRAL.

INT. MASTER BEDROOM - LIN HOUSE — NIGHT

A tripod screen is set up at the end of
the bed. There's a home movie projector
on Leo's night table. Leo threads cellu-
loid film from one reel of the projector
onto the other. Margaret sits patiently
in bed. Leo turns the projector on, then
bounds onto his side of the bed.

>   LEO
>   (expectantly)
>   Ready?

                        MARGARET
                    (stifling a yawn)

Leo, do we have to watch it on my
late night? Couldn't we watch it
tomorrow, when I'm not so tired.

                          LEO

I thought Thursday was your late
night. Today's Friday.

                        MARGARET

I switched days. (quickly) With my
co-worker.

                          LEO
               (in a slightly wheedling voice)

What in the world could have made
you so tired?

                        MARGARET

I told you. I worked late.

                          LEO

What kind of "*work*"?

Margaret looks at him puzzled. Leo turns
off the lamp on his night table. The
room is in total darkness except for the
FLICKERING of the film that's begun.

                          LEO

This is a very special movie.

> MARGARET

What about?

> LEO
> (with a sly smile)

You'll see.

SOUND of flicking tape. SOUNDS of moans
and groans come from the projector.
C.U. of Margaret's face as its expression gradually changes from weariness to
repulsion.

> MARGARET
> (trying to conceal her disgust;
> pleading)

Leo, the children. It'll wake the
children.

> LEO
> (engrossed, becoming sexually
> excited)

Shh. Just watch.

Leo begins to fondle Margaret, his eyes
all the while on the film.

> MARGARET
> (cringes, moves away)

Leo… No. Not now. Not like this.

>   LEO
>   (kissing her)
>
> Why not now? What better time than
> now? Or did you have enough — at
> "work"?

>   MARGARET
>   (pushing him away)
>
> Turn it off. Please, Leo. It'll wake
> the children.

>   LEO
>   (with growing anger)
>
> The children. That's all you care
> about.

SOUNDS of moaning and groaning from the
projector increase in frequency and in-
tensity. LIGHT from the pornographic
images of entwined bodies, naked women,
copulating couples projected onto the
screen flickers onto Leo and Margaret.

>   LEO
>   (contemptuously, all the while
>   kissing MARGARET, or trying to)
>
> No. Actually, your work comes first.
> Then the girls. And me? Where do
> I come in? Me! Your husband. Your
> HUSBAND!

He grabs her roughly, accidentally tearing the bodice of her nightgown.

Margaret pushes Leo off and runs out of
the room. She flings open Denise and Lorraine's bedroom door and climbs into bed
with Lorraine where she curls into a fe-
tal position.

                    LORRAINE
          (stirs)
     Mom? Mommy?

Sobbing uncontrollably, Margaret puts
her arms around Lorraine and her head in
her daughter's lap and holds her close.
Awakened, Denise looks over at her mother and sister. When Leo appears in the
doorway, Denise hides her head under her
covers. We see Leo only as a SILHOUETTE
in the doorway.

                    LEO
     Come back to the bedroom.

Margaret clings tighter to Lorraine and
shakes her head no. Denise pulls the
covers higher over her head. Lorraine
starts to cry.

                    LEO
          (threateningly)
     Margaret. Come with me. NOW.

Margaret shakes her head again, this
time more vigorously. Lorraine clasps
Margaret tightly to her.

> **LORRAINE**
> Don't go, Mommy. Don't go.

> **DENISE**
> (whispering to herself under
> the covers)
> Our Father Who art in heaven, hal-
> lowed by thy name. Thy Kingdom come.
> Thy will be done on earth as it is
> in heaven.

Leo strides to Lorraine's bedside and
grabs Margaret by the arm.

> **LEO**
> You'll come with me. NOW!

Leo pulls Margaret up. Lorraine holds
onto Margaret tighter.

> **MARGARET**
> (struggling to free herself of
> LEO)
> Leo! No! No! I won't!

> **LORRAINE**
> Daddy, no! Stop! Leave her alone!
> (pushes against LEO) LEAVE. HER.
> ALONE.

> **DENISE**
> (under her covers, louder, to
> drown out their voices)

> Give us this day our daily bread
> and forgive us our trespasses as we
> forgive those who trespass against
> us. And deliver us from evil. Amen.

Lorraine jumps out of bed and begins to
pummel Leo with her fists, forcing him to
retreat. She is FURY unbound.

                    LORRAINE
          Get out! Get out! GET OUT!

Shocked by Lorraine's behavior — and re-
volted by his own — Leo backs out of the
room with each blow until he's in the
hallway, then he rushes back to the master bedroom.

                    LORRAINE
            (standing in her bedroom door-
            way)
          I hate you! I HATE YOU!

INT. MASTER BEDROOM

Leo opens his desk drawer and grabs a
LETTER OPENER. Gripping it like a dagger,
he rushes to Margaret's clothes closet
and opens the door, accidentally swivel-
ing the home movie projector so that it
projects the lurid images onto his body.
He begins stabbing Margaret's Chinese
dresses with the letter opener, tearing them to shreds. He grunts and groans

with anguish and effort simultaneous with
the sighs and moans of the flickering film.

INT. DENISE AND LORRAINE'S BEDROOM

Denise huddles under her covers, muffling
her sobs. Lorraine sits on her bed with
Margaret — who lies Pietà-like across
her lap — and tenderly strokes her mother's hair.

INT. MASTER BEDROOM — NEXT MORNING

C.U. of the open SUITCASE filled with
Prudie's medals, plaques, awards, etc.
on the bed. Margaret sits beside it,
wistfully sifting through its contents.
Her Chinese dresses that Leo tore to
shreds the night before are strewn upon
the floor where he left them. The home
movie projector is still on the night
stand. The bed is unmade. When she hears
footsteps approaching, she slams the
suitcase shut just before Leo opens the
door. He enters the bedroom. He looks
awful, like he hasn't slept for days.

                    LEO
          (glances at SUITCASE, nods
          knowingly, wearily)
      I see. She never liked me.

>   MARGARET
>   (puzzled)
>
> Pru… Your daughter?

>   LEO
>
> Your MOTHER.

>   MARGARET
>   (catching on)
>
> She was afraid of you. No. Afraid's
> the wrong word. AWED. She was in
> awe of you. Her son-in-law whose
> father's a national living treasure.

>   LEO
>
> WAS. It's not the same thing. WAS a
> national living treasure. (bitter-
> ly) I'm the IS. The son of a WAS.
> And forever will be.

>   MARGARET
>   (trying to lighten the situa-
>   tion)
>
> Remember the first time she met your
> father? She asked me if she had to
> kowtow to him. She was afraid once
> she knelt down she wouldn't be able
> to get back up again.

>   LEO
>   (succumbing to her attempt at
>   levity)
>
> How about our first banquet in
> Shanghai? In your honor. You didn't

know how to shell the salt-baked
shrimps with your teeth. You ate
them, shells and all.

             MARGARET
Did I? Did I really? There was so
much to learn. The language. The
customs. The…

               LEO
You hated it.

             MARGARET
          (irked)
I LOVED it.

Margaret stands, goes to her jewelry box,
and opens it.

               LEO
       (semi-accusing, semi-joking)
You're a simple girl from Staten
Island.

             MARGARET
          (imperiously)
WAS. Who became a Shanghai
socialite.

She looks through the jewelry box and
frowns to find the JADE CICADA missing.
She looks knowingly towards Denise and
Lorraine's bedroom.

                    MARGARET
               (wistful)
     The Bund. Nanking Road. Dancing
     at the Cathay Hotel. The sundaes
     at the Chocolate Shop. The glamor-
     ous women. The suave men. (looks at
     LEO) You supported me every step of
     the way. Even to defying your fa-
     ther. He threatened to disown you
     if you married me. (smiles ruefully)
     He kept his word.

                      LEO
     When Pru… when our first child was
     born, he relented. By the time the
     other two came along, he and I'd
     reconciled. More or less.

                    MARGARET
     He never quite forgave me for hav-
     ing three girls. For not giving him
     grandsons.

                      LEO
     You're being selfish.

                    MARGARET
               (taken aback)
     Me? You think *I'm* the one who's
     selfish? I was happy just to have
     three healthy babies — boys *or*
     girls.

> LEO

That's not what I mean. I mean, you can't leave.

Margaret looks at the suitcase and puts two and two together.

> MARGARET

You thought I…

> LEO

How will the girls get to school from your mother's house? (disparagingly) On Staten Island.

> MARGARET
> (crosses her arms over her chest)

Yes, it's true that my family's not as educated or cultivated as yours. You married a dressmaker's daughter. A girl who attended design school. A TRADE school. (miffed, uncrosses her arms) Their education. Always their education! For once can you think of them as children and not Ph.D. candidates?

> LEO

I *am* thinking of them. It's *you* who are not.

                    MARGARET
          (incensed)
ME!

                    LEO
You're staying.

                    MARGARET
Is that an order?

                    LEO
I'M the one who's leaving. Tonight.

Margaret is stunned speechless.

                    LEO
          (looking at the SUITCASE)
There's no reason why you and the
girls should go. You have your job.
The girls have a week or two of
school left. I'll leave.

                    MARGARET
          (concerned)
Where will you go?

                    LEO
A motel. Until I can find an apartment for Nai-nai and me.

                    MARGARET
          (still disoriented, concerned)
You've been thinking about this —
for how long?

                    LEO

Long enough. Since last night.

                 MARGARET

Nai-nai's vegetable gardens. You
can't separate her from her gardens.

Leo's eyes soften; he stands taller; his
expression is hopeful, expectant.

                 MARGARET

There's no reason why *she* can't
stay.

Leo's face crumples; his body sags. Horror-stricken at what she's just said,
Margaret sucks in her breath.

                    LEO
             (witheringly)

That's generous of you.

The PHONE on the night stand rings. Margaret collects herself before answering
it.

                 MARGARET
            (into the receiver)

Hello. Lin residence.

               EVELYN (O.S.)

Margaret dear. It's Evelyn.

                    MARGARET
               (looking at LEO)
          Hello, Evelyn.

     Leo freezes.

                    EVELYN (O.S.)
          This coming Sunday is the first Sun-
          day of the month. As if I need re-
          mind you. Can we expect you for
          dinner? As usual.

                    MARGARET
               (still looking at LEO)
          Yes. We'll be there. As usual.

                    EVELYN (O.S.)
          We-ll, not exactly 'as usual.' It's
          Guoxin's birthday. I'm sure Leo
          told you.

                    MARGARET
          Of course he did. His father's
          birthday is this Sunday.

                    EVELYN (O.S.)
          Actually, Guoxin's birthday is on
          Tuesday. But we're celebrating
          it two days early. For YOUR sake.
          Working woman that you are.

                    MARGARET
          That's very considerate of you.

                         EVELYN (O.S.)
Not at all. (sarcastically) We're
family. Till Sunday. One o'clock.

                         MARGARET
One o'clock.

CLICK of the receiver on Evelyn's end.
Margaret hangs up. Dejected, Leo slumps
down into his desk chair.

                           LEO
I can't leave. Not now. I'll have
to wait till after this Sunday. Until then, everything will be as it
was. (agitated) He mustn't know.
My father must never know. In fact,
nobody must know. Not a word to our
neighbors.

                         MARGARET
                       (deadpan)

Leo. We never speak to our neighbors as it is.

                           LEO
                    (self-righteously)

And with good reason. (opening
and slamming desk drawer repeated-
ly) Gossip. (SLAM) Scandal. (SLAM)
That's all they're interested in.
(SLAM) Who do they think they are
(SLAM) — telling me how to trim MY
trees!

MARGARET

You won't even let the girls have
their school friends over.

LEO

So they can interfere with their
homework? They see their friends
at school. Why do they have to
see them at home? (rises from desk
chair) I know. I'll leave in the
morning and return in the evening.
That way the neighbors won't suspect a thing. I'll sleep in the
guest room. I'll eat my meals out.
No one will be the wiser. And you
won't even know I'm here. (starts
to leave the room; stops on the
threshold) Oh. About the Chinese
dresses…

Margaret looks up at Leo expectantly.

LEO

…they wouldn't fit you now anyway.

CUT

It's musical chairs—only in reverse, Denise decided as she sat down to dinner. *Instead of a chair being taken away, it's a person. First it was Prudie.* She glanced at her sister's place setting at the dining room table, her empty chair. *And now it's Daddy.* She eyeballed his empty place, his vacant chair to the right of the head of the table— that honored spot he relinquished to his mother upon her arrival.

Raised pre-Nai-nai on American food set on platters passed around the table, Denise had grown accustomed post-Nai-nai to stationary platters of Chinese food to which she stretched out her arm and unhygienically plucked, again and again, a morsel with her chopsticks and carried it back to her bowl of boiled white rice. One thing that hadn't changed with Prudie's disappearance, or Nai-nai's arrival, Denise noted, was the family's habit of eating in near total silence. Would her father's absence tonight shatter—or reinforce—the Lin tradition of eating and digesting undisturbed by conversation? Silence interrupted only by the clink of chopsticks against rice bowls, an indiscreet burp or two from Nai-nai, a few mournful whimpers from Bert at the foot of Lorraine's chair? Infuriating, suffocating silence?

"Why isn't Daddy having dinner with us?" Denise asked in a tone of voice that demanded to know.

Margaret reached across the table and plucked a piece of egg scrambled with minced *lap-cheung* with her chopsticks. It gave her a few seconds to think of how she might answer.

"He's eating out."

"How come?"

"He didn't say."

"It's because of last night," Lorraine quipped, emboldened, "isn't it?"

Margaret was silent, which her daughters understood as involuntarily giving assent. She was also discomfited. Denise could see she was—by the way her mother pressed her lips together, by the stiffness of her spine, especially her neck, when she brought the morsel of food in her chopsticks to her mouth, by how carefully she chewed it. Denise bristled internally, thrilled that the despotic rulers of the Lin household—silence, compliance (or lip service, as the case might be, and often was), propriety, platitudes—had been ousted, creating a power vacuum into which words now rushed in. Worse than words. Questions. Questions requiring, *demanding*, answers.

"Is he leaving us?" Denise said.

"Of course not," Margaret said, too quickly.

An image/thought appeared in Denise's mind's eye. It was a picture/metaphor of that counterintuitive Chinese trick where you inserted your forefingers into the two ends of a thin tube of woven bamboo. The harder you pulled your fingers apart to try to release them, the tighter the tube gripped them. The more she questioned her mother, the more her mother sought to evade answering her. The more her mother sought to evade answering, the tighter she was caught in the constricting tube, trapped into answering, forced to lie.

"But if he *does* leave," Lorraine emphasized, "just *if*, will he be taking Nai-nai with him?"

Ah! Denise thought, gloating. *No more carrying Bert's night soil to fertilize her vegetables. Normal food again. Now that Mom's working, maybe even frozen dinners. And* finally *I get Prudie's room.*

Margaret set down her chopsticks and leaned forward in her chair. But instead of pushing it back, rising to her feet and leaving the table to avoid answering, as Denise anticipated, her mother sat upright at the edge of her seat and looked calmly, even *formally*, at her daughters.

"Daddy's not leaving. That is, he's not leaving until after Sunday. How long he'll be away, I don't know. He didn't say."

They heard the click of the key in the back door lock and, a few seconds later, the door opening, then shutting, and the chain guard sliding into place.

"Daddy's home," Lorraine whispered.

The door to Margaret's sewing room (infrequently used ever since she began working) which also served as a guest room (seldom used as such, ever) whined open and, a few seconds later, was gently but firmly shut.

"Daddy's ghost, you mean," Denise whispered back.

"Until then, Daddy will be using the guest room," Margaret continued, seamlessly. "He'll be gone for most of the day. If you do see him—*when* you see him—remember that he's your father. He deserves your respect. That includes keeping up your Mandarin lessons. Your tai qi, Lorraine. And your calligraphy, Denise. Soon you'll be on summer vacation. You'll have lots of time to practice both."

My food's cold, Denise noticed, swallowing a bit of soy sauce chicken. *Talking at table did that. Lets your food get cold. Words coming out of our mouths, and nothing going into them.*

Her eyes followed Nai-nai who stood up and walked to the kitchen table. She picked up a tray set with a bowl and a plate of food—both covered to keep them warm—and carried it in the direction of the guest room, out of Denise's sight. Denise heard the three soft raps on the guest room door, the several seconds of

silence that ensued, and then Leo's Chinese name. *Lei-hou.* It was
the first word Nai-nai had spoken since sitting down to dinner.
When there was no answer, she repeated it, then, "*Ni chi le fan le
ma?*" It was one of the first sentences Denise and Lorraine learned
in Mandarin. "Have you eaten yet?" It also doubled as a greeting
among familiars, similar to "How are you doing?"

"I saved some dinner for you," Denise heard her grandmother
say. The words traveled, in part due the reverberation of the closed
guest room door, in part due to the fact that Nai-nai, her hearing
not what it used to be, sometimes shouted instead of spoke. "It's
still warm. Or I could heat it up for you."

Silence. Then, barely audibly: "Take it away. I've already eaten."

Or was that what Denise, hearing only an indistinct mumble, a
distant vibration, put into her father's mouth?

Through the open doorway, Denise watched her grandmother
return to the kitchen, set the spurned dinner back on the Formica
table top, and gaze out the window above the sink at the lilac bushes
in full bloom—bushes that had escaped Leo's horticultural ardor.
Though she was physically lighter by the tray of food she'd been
carrying, Nai-nai seemed to bear on her sagging shoulders a weight
far greater than the small burden she'd just set down.

That night, Denise lies in bed, staring at the shadows cast on her venetian blind by the shorn stinkweed tree. In her mind, images form, deform, dissolve, and disappear, replaced by others whose fate is the same. Some of them have nothing to do with the sumac's shadows (the Magic Pictures) drawn by sumac branches (the Magic Crayons) on the venetian blind (the Magic Window). For example, the fairytale *The Princess and the Pea* that surfaces unbidden from the depths of her conscience. *I am not the princess,* Denise assures herself. *And the jade cicada I've "borrowed" from my mother's jewelry box and put under my mattress "temporarily, for safe keeping" is not the pea that keeps the fairytale princess tossing and turning at night, unable to sleep, despite the twelve mattresses between her delicate body and that distant, irritating pea. The Princess and the Pea is not interfering with, has nothing to do with, Winky Dink and You,* she intones silently.

Denise closes her eyes to erase the princess's pea from her thoughts. When she opens them again, it is in the hope that she'll see her Magic Window and its Magic Pictures—the venetian blind and the shadows cast on it by the *ailanthus altissima*. Ah. Success. A clean screen with some blotchy shadows. She stares into mid-space to expand her peripheral vision. She knows by now that focusing too hard will only make the branches branches, the leaves leaves, reality merely reality. She lies still. She breathes breaths that are long, slow, and silent. She knows she will, in time, be rewarded by surrendering her efforts to be effortless.

In time, she is. The movie playing tonight is a rerun featuring the same beetle-browed giant—sitting in profile, knees pulled up against his chest, arms wrapped around his shins—who filled her entire screen weeks ago. And here, as before, comes the protagonist, the same tiny female carrying the same heavy sack upon her back, trudging up the shallow steps of his vertebrae. But whereas the previous movie stopped mid-dream, this, its sequel, continues where its predecessor left off. The girl laboriously scales the giant's neck, the back of his skull, crosses over the crown of his head, rappels down the sheer cliff of his forehead and the sharp outcropping of his nose, to the narrow crevice between his lips. She sets down her burden on his lower lip, opens the sack, and withdraws its precious contents. She pries open the giant's lips and with great effort pushes the tongue of jade inside.

"SPEAK! SPEAK!" she cries into the big black cave of his resounding mouth.

Denise sits bolt upright in bed. She's sweating—the warm perspiration of physical exertion, not the cold rank sweat of fear. Her breathing is labored. Her ears are ringing from the echo of her shout, her throat sore from it. Something is in the air. A scent. A familiar odor. Pleasurable. Sensual. It draws her out of bed and leads her down the stairs to the kitchen. The light is on. She stops on the threshold. Her father, dressed in his pajamas, stands at the stove hovering over a pot of boiling water. Gently, he presses a handful of dry spaghetti against the bottom of the pot so that, as it softens, it will fan out and separate into individual strands. A cast iron skillet rests on the low flame of the adjacent burner. The kitchen table is set with a ceramic bowl, a pair of bamboo chopsticks, a plate of leftovers from dinner, and an open jar of something light brown, or gray.

Leo turns his head, acknowledging Denise's presence just barely. He doesn't seem to be surprised to see her. Nor is Denise surprised to see him. She steps inside the kitchen. The linoleum feels smooth and cool on the soles of her bare feet. He swirls the spaghetti around with a wooden spoon.

"I can't sleep," she says. "What are you making?"

"Chinese food," he says, dolloping a tablespoon of congealed chicken fat into the skillet.

"Smells good."

"Get another bowl. And a pair of chopsticks. And another egg from the refrigerator."

Leo lights another burner, sets a second, larger skillet on it, and adds a tablespoon of chicken fat to that one as well. Denise does as she's told, then sits at the kitchen table. She watches her father add more spaghetti to the pot of boiling water, deftly break one egg, then the second, into the smaller skillet. Both yolks remain unbroken, she notices, the whites miraculously almost circular. While the eggs sputter and bubble, Leo empties the plate of leftovers into the remaining skillet. The meat and vegetables crackle and hiss. Denise spears a cube from inside the jar on the kitchen table with one of her chopsticks and inspects the specimen closely.

"What's this? It's got the same consistency as the thick white paste we used for art projects in grammar school." She thinks of adding that it's also that crayon-box color *taupe*, named for the blah color of the mammal's fur, but she reconsiders the urge and restrains herself. Instead, she brings the jar chose to her nose, which wrinkles in disgust. "It smells like a dead animal. A *small* dead animal," she says, concession to her father's disapproving glance for her impertinent remark which is followed by his slightly raised eyebrows, indication that it's beneath his dignity to acknowledge her statement with a verbal response.

Leo drains the cooked spaghetti in the sink, then fills each bowl with the noodles, meat, and vegetables and slides a fried egg on top. The yolks glisten like polished jewels. He sets one bowl in front of Denise, the other at his place at table opposite her. He picks up a cube of whatever occupies the open jar with his chopsticks and places it on the rim of his bowl where it adheres.

It even sticks like paste, Denise observes.

"What is it?" she ventures.

Leo lances his egg yolk. Denise watches the viscous liquid seep into his rice and leftovers.

"*Foo yee*. Fermented bean curd." He scrapes the tip of his chopsticks against the taupe-colored cube and swabs the pea-sized dab of *foo yee* on his first bite of food which he eats with undisguised relish.

"Maybe I'll try some. Just a little bit."

"You won't like it." A statement. A warning. A dare.

Leo captures almost half of his fermented bean curd cube between his chopsticks and smears it on the rim of Denise's bowl, then returns to his single-minded pursuit of gastronomic pleasure. Denise joins him with equal gusto. Even to swabbing a bit of *foo yee*—very salty, slightly bitter, musty, metallic—on each mouthful of food. Even to masticating vigorously, feeling the muscles of her jaw working to eke every iota of flavor from her food.

They eat avidly, their wordlessness a vacuum into which rush the convivial clink of bamboo chopsticks against ceramic bowl, the languid hum of the small rotating fan next to the dish rack, the hypnotic rasp of the cicadas through the open kitchen windows. Enough said.

INT. ST. PATRICK'S CATHEDRAL -
A FEW DAYS LATER

Leo sits in one of the front pews — empty but for him — reading from a thick black BOOK. Two PRIESTS walk down the aisle past him.

>   PRIEST #1
>   (to PRIEST #2)
>
> Did you notice that Oriental man?
> He comes here almost every weekday
> and reads from his missal. (nods
> knowingly) The power of faith, Father Laughlin. The power of faith.

>   PRIEST #2
>
> I've always found it to be true: a
> Catholic born and bred can't hold a
> candle to a heathen convert when it
> comes to unquestioning devotion.

C.U. of the book Leo is reading. The title on the cover reads TANG DYNASTY POETRY. C.U. of the poem he is reading entitled "To my daughter on her marriage into the Yang family" by Wei Ying-wu. C.U. of the stanza:

>   My heart has been heavy all day
>   long
>   Because you have so far to go.
>   The marriage of a girl, away
>   from her parents,

Is the launching of a little
boat on a great river.
... After this morning we separate,
There's no knowing for how
long...
I always try to hide my feelings —
They are suddenly too much for
me,
When I turn and see my younger
daughter
With the tears running down her
cheek.

Leo leaves the pew and walks to the
front of the nave where he stands before
the statue of Christ Crucified. He stares
up at Christ's tormented face.

                    LEO
What kind of father would allow
his only son to be reviled, tor-
tured, and put to death? For sins
he didn't commit. And call it love.

EXT. LIN HOUSE — SUNDAY, EARLY AFTERNOON

To the sound of the DRUM ROLL preceding execution by firing squad, first Lorraine (glum), followed by Denise (dour),
then Margaret (forbearing), and finally
Leo (tense) — all in their Sunday best

— march single file and in lock step from the front door to the family car and get inside. Katrinka back-fires a few times before the engine turns over. Looking out the living room window, Bert howls plaintively at each retort. Nai-nai stands next to Bert watching her family leave.

INT. GUOXIN'S DINING ROOM — TWO HOURS LATER

C.U. of the SIXTY CANDLES on Guoxin's birthday cake which he blows out after a few concerted tries. Oohs and aahs and polite applause from Evelyn, Leo, Margaret, Denise, Lorraine and Aiying the cook.

                    GUOXIN
          (to AIYING, in Mandarin)
     Dinner was excellent. It took all
     my will power to save some room for
     dessert.

Aiying smiles and nods.

                    EVELYN
          (to AIYING, in Mandarin)
     Did you put the gifts where I told
     you?

                              AIYING
                        (in Mandarin)

               Yes, Madam. In the living room. On
               the coffee table.

                              EVELYN
                        (in Mandarin)

               We'll eat our cake there. No tea.
               Just champagne. I put two magnums
               of Taittinger in the refrigerator.
               Set out four champagne flutes. No.
               Five.

                              AIYING
                        (in Mandarin)

               Yes, Madam.

          Aiying exits.

                              EVELYN
                   (to GUOXIN, LEO, MARGARET, DE-
                   NISE and LORRAINE)

               Shall we have our cake and eat it
               too? In the living room.

          They all push their chairs back from the
          table and get to their feet.

     INT. GUOXIN'S LIVING ROOM —
     A FEW MINUTES LATER

          Both Lin families are seated around
          the coffee table set with an ice bucket

containing two champagne bottles, champagne flutes, and plates of birthday cake.
Guoxin, Evelyn, Denise, and Lorraine sit
on the sofa. Leo and Margaret sit opposite each other in armchairs. The TV is
turned on, but the volume is off. Guoxin pops the cork on one of the champagne
bottles. Oohs and aahs. He fills the five
flutes. Aiying passes to everyone except
Lorraine. Denise hesitates before accepting the flute. When Leo scowls at her,
she looks away.

                    EVELYN
          (raises her flute to GUOXIN)
     Sheng ri kuai le! Happy Birthday!

               LEO, MARGARET, DENISE,
               LORRAINE
     Sheng ri kuai le!

All sip from their flutes. Evelyn takes
one of the gift-wrapped boxes from the
coffee table and shakes it near her ear.

                    EVELYN
     Let me guess. An article of cloth-
     ing. That means it can only be from
     Margaret. From that department
     store where you work, am I right,
     and get a steep discount?

Margaret smiles stiffly and takes another
sip of champagne.

                    EVELYN

It must save you a LOT of money.
Dressing your three girls must cost
a FORTUNE. What a shame that Prudence couldn't make it home for her
grandfather's sixtieth birthday!
Such an important occasion. (to DE-
NISE) Drink. Drink! You're a growing girl.

Denise finishes her glass. Evelyn quickly
refills it, despite a gesture of protes-
tation from Leo. Denise takes a big gulp.

                    EVELYN

Ah! That's what I like to see!
(hands the gift to GUOXIN, who begins to unwrap the box) I bet it's
a sweater. A cardigan. Another one.

It is.

                   GUOXIN
                (to MARGARET)

Xie-xie. Xie-xie. (Thank you. Thank
you.)

                   MARGARET

Bu keqi. (You're welcome.)

                    EVELYN
            (feeling the sweater between
            thumb and forefinger)
Orlon?

                    MARGARET
            (cooly)
Cashmere. One hundred per cent.

                    LEO
            (to DENISE)
That's enough.

                    DENISE
            (tipsy, holds the flute on high)
Gan bei! (Bottoms up!)

                    EVELYN
Yes, yes! (toasts) *Gan bei! Gan
bei!*

All drain their flutes.

                    EVELYN
            (fingers the sweater again; to
            MARGARET)
Two ply?

                    MARGARET
Three.

                    EVELYN
            (feigning surprise)
Three. Really?

                    LEO
          (cautioning, to MARGARET)
     Margaret…

                  MARGARET
          (ignores him; to EVELYN with
           restrained ire)
     Made in Hong Kong.

                  EVELYN
     Ah! (dismissively) The British
     crown colony. The only place for
     good cashmere sweaters is Shanghai.
     WAS Shanghai. I do hope it's the
     right size. My husband is a medium.

     Margaret is about to respond when…

                    LEO
          (to GUOXIN, in Mandarin)
     Your granddaughters have something
     to give you too.

                  GUOXIN
          (eyes lighting up)
     Zhende? (Really?)

     Leo gets up and gestures for Denise to
     help him move the coffee table. She's
     unsteady on her feet, and her movements
     are clumsy and awkward.

                    LEO
          (whispering to DENISE)
     Are you ready?

DENISE nods.

                    LEO
     Remember — nothing less than
     perfection.

Denise stands in front of the gathering,
empty flute in hand, swaying slightly.

                    DENISE
     Drinking Alone with the Moon, by Li
     Po. I'll pretend that this (holds
     up the champagne flute) is the moon.
     And I'll pretend that I'm the poet
     Li Po. They say that Li Po was a
     drunkard. (twirls the flute in her
     hand) Now I see why he was able to
     write such incredible poetry. So
     here goes nothing…

Thanks to the champagne, Denise is unin-
hibited, pronouncing the words perfectly
in Mandarin, enunciating them to dramat-
ic effect, and gesturing grandly as ine-
briated Li Po might well have done, including slurring some of his words. Her
audience, however, is in shock. Margaret,
humiliated for her daughter, shuts her
eyes. Guoxin, confused and embarrassed,

looks away. Evelyn titters malicious-
ly behind her raised hand. Lorraine's
jaw drops. She stares at Denise as if
she's seeing an utter — but interesting
— stranger. Leo, appalled, grinds his
teeth until Denise concludes the poem
and his agony is finally over.

> LEO
> (jumps to his feet, clapping
> loudly)

Hao. Hen hao. (pulls DENISE towards
the sofa) That's enough. (whispers angrily in her ear) What's
wrong with you! You made a fool
of yourself. At your grandfather's
birthday.

> DENISE
> (frees herself from LEO)

I'm not done yet. There's more.
There's BETTER. I want to recite
this poem by Paul Verlaine. In
French. (dramatically) *Il pleure
dans mon coeur comme il pleut sur
la ville.*

Evelyn gasps, recites with Denise.

                    DENISE AND EVELYN
                    (simultaneously)

        Quelle est cette langueur qui
        pénètre mon coeur?

                         DENISE
                  (surprised, to EVELYN)

        Mais vous parlez français! [But you
        speak French!]

Leo succeeds in prodding Denise to the
sofa.

                         EVELYN

        *Et pourquoi pas? J'ai fait mes
        études à la Conservatoire à Par-
        is. Avec Nadia Boulanger. Pendant
        deux ans. Assieds-toi. Ici, près
        de moi.* [And why not? I studied at
        the Paris Conservatory. With Nadia
        Boulanger. For two years. Sit here,
        next to me.]

Denise sits beside Evelyn, who takes her
hand and holds it.

                         EVELYN

        *J'aime Paul Verlaine. Beaucoup.
        Surtout ce poème.* [I love Paul Ver-
        laine. Very much. Especially this

poem.]

                    DENISE
                (ecstatic)

O moi aussi. Moi aussi! [Oh, me too.
Me too!]

                    EVELYN

*Il me fait rappeller de mon sé-
jour à Paris. Quand j'étais jeune.*
(looks accusingly at GUOXIN) *Et
heureuse.* [It reminds me of my stay
in Paris. When I was young. And
happy.]

Leo pulls Lorraine off the couch and has
her stand before the gathering. Lorraine
shrinks into herself.

                    LEO
                (to LORRAINE)

Okay, you're next. Stand up
straight. (whispers in her ear)
Make me proud of you. Show everyone
I have one daughter I don't have to
be ashamed of.

Leo takes his seat and gestures for Lorraine to begin.

                    LORRAINE
                (nervously)

Sheng ri kuai le, Grampa. I've been
learning tai qi…

Leo cups his hands around his mouth.

                      LEO
                (in a whisper)

Say it in Mandarin. In Mandarin.

                    LORRAINE
             (distracted, confused)

…and I was going to perform the
twenty-four steps for your birthday.
But they just didn't…

Leo practically rises out of his chair
and continues to mouth "In Mandarin,"
but Lorraine is too nervous to understand and continues speaking in English.

                    LORRAINE

…seem happy enough for a happy sixtieth birthday. So this is what I
want to give you instead. I hope
you like it.

Lorraine whips out a copy of Mao's LIT-
TLE RED BOOK and, to everyone's horror —
but Denise's delight — and the imagined
accompaniment of a full orchestra and
chorus, she begins to sing and perform

the LOYALTY DANCE. Before she can finish,
Guoxin rises to his feet.

> GUOXIN
> (always in Mandarin)

Stop! STOP!

Lorraine, confused, stops singing and
dancing. Leo, stunned, rises slowly to
his feet.

> GUOXIN
> (to LEO)

What do you think you're doing?

> LEO
> (in Mandarin from here to end
> of scene)

I had no idea that she was going to
change her program from tai…

> GUOXIN
> (trembling with rage)

Is this how you celebrate my sixtieth birthday? By insulting me?

> LEO
> (contrite)

I had no idea that she'd changed
her gift to you. It's my fault. I
should have monitored her — both my
daughters — more closely.

                         GUOXIN
     What kind of daughters have
     you raised? A bunch of juvenile
     delinquents!

Leo shrinks at each denigrating remark
as Guoxin's words become even more de-
rogatory and hurtful.

                         GUOXIN
     One is an alcoholic. The other is a
     Chinese Communist. And the third is
     off in California becoming a beach
     bum or a beatnik — probably both.
     Why should I have expected any bet-
     ter. From YOU. A (contemptuously)
     merchant. All your life you've nev-
     er been anything but a disappoint-
     ment to me. But when you married
     that foreign devil of a wife…

                         LEO
                    (explodes)
     You, you of all people, have no
     right to say that. To say ANYTHING
     about Margaret. You aren't even
     worthy to say her name.

                       MARGARET
                 (frightened, to DENISE)
     What did they say about me? What's
     Daddy saying?

                    DENISE
          (riveted by LEO and GUOXIN's
          verbal battling)

I don't know, exactly. Grampa
doesn't approve of us. Not any of
us. But Daddy defended you.

                    LEO
          (seething, but trying to con-
          trol himself)

Not when you, YOU of all people… You have NO RIGHT! Yes, I'm
a businessman. A merchant. WAS. If
I hadn't been, you couldn't have
lived like this.

                   GUOXIN
          (taken aback)

That's enough. How dare you speak
to me like this, in my house.

                    LEO

You call the money I give you
"filthy." But you accept it. Not from
me. Oh, no! Not face to face. Margaret has to slip it to you — behind your back. And then, only then,
do you condescend to accept it. And
how you glory in the fact that I
let you demean her. That I let you
humiliate her. That I don't have
the backbone to stuff the money down
your…into your hands myself. You

enjoy that, don't you? And why? Because Margaret is a *guailou*. A foreign devil. And I had the guts to
marry her — against your wishes!

             GUOXIN
        (fists clenched, shaking with
        rage)

Get out of my house. This is MY
house. Get out!

             LEO

NOT BEFORE YOU TELL ME WHO NATASHA
WAS. WHO WAS SHE? TELL ME!

Evelyn, drained of all color, rises, goes over to the piano and begins
to play Debussy's *Clair de Lune*. Denise
follows her and sits beside her on the
piano bench. Guoxin glares at Evelyn.
She ignores him.

             GUOXIN
        (caustic, spiteful)

Natasha? The woman I left your
mother for? (looks at EVELYN) The
only woman I've ever loved?

Evelyn winces, but plays on, plays
louder.

             LEO

Why did you marry my mother?

GUOXIN

How American you are, Leo! You married Margaret (disparagingly) for
love. By doing so, you were will-
ing to estrange me. Which you did.
I married for HONOR. I married your
mother to honor my father's word.
To keep the promise he made to your
mother's father — my father's gardener. Which was to give his first
— and as it turned out, his only —
son in marriage to his gardener's
daughter.

LEO

An arranged marriage. That's nothing unusual, times being what they
were. But between a Mandarin schol-
ar and a simple gardener…

GUOXIN

Your mother's father saved my life.
Don't ask me how. Or why. Yes, he
was a gardener. But SIMPLE? (scoffs)
He was a master in his field. An
artist. As my father was in his.
Your mother and I were betrothed
when I was three years old. She was
fourteen.

                    LEO

And Natasha. (sarcastically) The
only woman you ever loved.

                    GUOXIN
            (helplessly, passionately)

Natasha.

                                   FADE OUT

Natasha. Natasha.

The more forcefully Evelyn struck the piano keys, the softer the sound of the notes. At least to Guoxin's ears.

Natasha. Natasha.

The name resounded in his mind, stirred his memory. *Clair de Lune* was waning and Evelyn was disappearing. Leo was fading. Then Margaret. And Denise. Lorraine. The piano. The dining room itself. His very house. The sylvan suburb where he lived. The country where he'd taken refuge. When he breathed, it was to the rhythm of her name. When his heart beat, it was to the syllables of her name.

Na Ta Sha. Na Ta Sha.

The sonority of her name! It was music itself. Not light, capricious Impressionistic French music but the deep, soulful music of her country. Named after the heroine of *War and Peace*, she was a White Russian. A foreign devil. A beautiful, high-strung pianist from St. Petersburg born into a family of artists and musicians fleeing their country during the Bolshevik Revolution and finding safe haven in Shanghai. She was just beginning to make a name for herself as a concert pianist in the "Paris of the Orient," but her renown as an incomparable beauty had preceded—and overtaken—her talent as a musician. It drew young (and old) men in droves who had little or no interest in listening to Rachmaninoff, Scriabin, and Tchaikovsky to hear and, especially, to see her play. Bachelor friends of Guoxin invited him to join them at one of her concerts. After much teasing and cajoling, they also succeeded in persuading him to accompany them backstage after the performance to pay their respects and present her with a flamboyant bouquet of flowers.

"C'mon, Guoxin. We need someone dignified and articulate to act as our spokesman. You're a poet from a good family. You'll know exactly how to act and what to say."

But Guoxin was at a loss for words the moment Natasha walked onto the stage. This state of confusion and longing continued for the entire length of her performance. He was similarly tongue-tied afterwards in her dressing room, despite his garrulous friends, but his eyes spoke eloquently where his voice was mute. More eloquently than his verbal or written poetry ever had been, ever *could* be, the sentiments they conveyed were easily translated by the woman to whom he'd unwittingly offered his heart. As his companions took their leave, she gestured for him to remain behind. After she closed the door, she drew a single flower from the bouquet they'd given her—the least showy, the least colorful, possessing the deepest calyx formed by the whorl of its single petal: a calla lily—and gave it to him.

They began to keep each other company. *En cachette* at first. Then, more and more frequently, they appeared together in public where it was assumed—and accepted—that Natasha was his mistress. He rented a house for her in the French Concession. He bought her a car and hired a chauffeur. He purchased her a wardrobe of custom-made clothes. She never played the piano again. Not professionally. Only for Guoxin and his closest friends.

Natasha. Natasha.

Guoxin heard Evelyn playing Debussy. It hurt his ears. More abrasive was the sound of Leo's voice demanding to know: And what about your father? And my mother?

Guoxin recalled both people, both reluctantly and wistfully.

Especially his father.

My father—for whom his gardener sacrificed five years of his own life in order to protect his employer—was in the self-same predicament where I, his son, would find myself years later. In love with an unsuitable woman. Ironic, no? But there are differences. In my father's case, the woman wasn't a guailou *but a young Chinese woman betrothed to another man. When her fiancé confronted my father and accused him of treachery and tampering with an innocent girl's feelings, my father lost his temper and struck him. The blow wasn't hard but it was forceful enough to cause the man to lose his balance, fall, and hit his head on a rock.*

A violent death caused by the master poet and calligrapher Lin Yu-tao. An accusation of murder. A scandal. Even if it were proven that the death was accidental, the violent blow was certainly not. Ostracism. Ruin. For the entire family. And so it was decided. My father's gardener, who had witnessed the confrontation, would take the blame. His story: he had tried to defend his employer when the jealous assailant attacked him. In the scuffle, he had struck the man, accidentally killing him.

Luckily, the jealous assailant was Chinese. Had he been Caucasian, the sentence would have been life. Even death. The trial was held in Mixed Court, where Shanghai's Chinese cases were tried, as opposed to Municipal Court, where the cases of Caucasians were adjudicated. The sentence was ten years. Because the Lin family was powerful and influential, the gardener—my father-in-law—served only five of them. I say 'only' tongue in cheek. My father was nothing if not honorable. He was a great believer in fairness and reciprocity. It was due to those two guiding principles that he promised his firstborn—should the child be a boy—in marriage to the gardener's daughter, who was eleven when I was born.

Guoxin remembered all of this in one instantaneous flash when Leo asked about his paternal grandfather and his own mother. But Guoxin shared none of it with his son. He said instead:

"I honored my commitment to your mother. I gave her the respect she was due as my first wife. As for my father, he wanted me to end what he thought was a short-lived infatuation. But when it continued and our bond only grew stronger, he threatened to cut off my allowance. I answered that I'd kept the promise that he had made in my name: I had married his gardener's daughter. I told him that I was in love with Natasha and would marry her if I could. I beseeched him not to make any more demands of me, and to make no more promises on my behalf. As for your father-in-law, never once did he mention my extramarital liaison. Neither did your mother. Not once. It went on like this for two years. Then one evening..."

Natasha. Natasha. Natasha. Natasha.

The word, the sound, her name. They were growing fainter while the images, the memories, the feelings grew stronger, more distinct.

"What is it?" Leo asked, troubled more by his father's vague expression than his lapse into silence.

"Your mother and I were having dinner at home. One of the servants came into the dining room to say that a house—a house built of red and black bricks—four blocks away was on fire. That description fit only one house that I knew of. I rose from the table and rushed out the door. I could smell the smoke even before I saw it. People were running and shouting. I heard the clanging of the fire engine bells in the distance. Then I knew that Natasha was fulfilling her promise—now that she was the mother of my son."

"Vladimir," Leo murmured.

"Vladimir," Guoxin echoed, barely a whisper. "Soon after he was born, Natasha began behaving strangely. Having tantrums. Crying fits. She'd always been high-strung. Nervous. Impetuous. But now, the slightest thing set her off. The doctor said some women became depressed following childbirth but that it would pass. One day, she told me she would set the house on fire if I didn't divorce your mother and marry her. She said she had no intention of remaining my concubine, as she called it, now that she had borne my son. I told her that I would marry her, that she would have second wife status and all its privileges. But she insisted I divorce your mother and marry her as my only wife. I said that was impossible. I told her I couldn't divorce your mother. I had given my father my word—or rather, my father had given your mother's father his word in my stead—and I would keep it."

Guoxin sat down on the sofa. His legs had given way. His body was a crumpled mass, a dead weight. But his memory, dislodged from his physical form, was effluent. Words coursed out of him unimpeded.

"I didn't believe she would carry it out. The way she said it—the fact that she was emotionless, even serene, when she said it—should have warned me otherwise. When I arrived at the house, it was in flames. Natasha and Vladimir were inside."

"How did you know?" Leo asked.

"Bystanders had seen them. Both of them. On the second floor. Through the window. When I heard that, I lost my mind. I ran towards the entrance gate. Someone, then another person, then a third, restrained me. I'm not a big man, but I found the strength to break free of them and push open the gate. "Vladimir!" I cried. "Natasha! Vladimir!" I tore off my jacket and held it over my face and chest to shield my body from the wall of fire consuming the front door. The heat was overpowering, the smoke blinding, suffocating, when I heard:

"Baba! Baba! Wo ai ni, Baba!"

"Vladimir," Leo murmured.

"Vladimir," Guoxin repeated, perplexed. "Vladimir was six months old. It was *you*. You and your mother had run out of our house after me. She was restraining you. You were trying to break free of her, holding out your arms to me while your mother clung to you and held you back."

'Baba! Baba! Wo ai ni, Baba!'

Leo began to tremble.

"To this day, I don't know if I wanted to save Natasha and our son, or if I wanted to die along with them. But you stopped me. Your presence. Your words. Your love. I don't know if I ever forgave you. How could I ever live up to the example you set for me? You saved my life. Perhaps it runs in the family," Guoxin said, a choking or chuckling noise caught in his throat. "Your mother's father saves my father's life. Then you save mine. And for what? So I could watch you achieve what I was incapable of. So I should relive my failure every time I look at you. At Margaret. At your daughters."

Leo staggered backwards, turned, and lurched towards the front door.

"Leo!" Margaret, rising to her feet, called after him. "Leo!"

By the time she, Denise, and Lorraine reached the front door, Leo had crossed the hump-backed bridge. In seconds he was inside Katrinka, revving the motor, backing out of the clearing, and careening onto the road leading to the highway. When Margaret and her two daughters reached the near end of the footbridge, Katrinka was nowhere in sight.

"Here."

Margaret turned around and came face to face with Evelyn.

Evelyn took her hand and dropped a set of keys into her palm. "Take my car..." She glanced at the black Mercedes-Benz sedan at the far end of the footbridge, then furled Margaret's fingers around the keys with both her hands.

"But you. Guoxin…"

"Hurry. You must catch up with your husband. Don't worry about us. We'll be fine. Now we'll be fine."

EXT. LIN HOUSE - LATE AFTERNOON

Leo speeds towards home. He glances out
the windshield at the huge yellow SUN.
FADE to Prudie as a little girl sitting
in the back of the car looking out the
rearwindow while Leo is driving.

                    PRUDIE AS LITTLE GIRL
          Look, Daddy! The sun loves me.

                    LEO
          Why do you say that?

                    PRUDIE AS LITTLE GIRL
          Because it's following me. It wants
          to be near me.

BLAST of a car horn, as Leo veers towards another lane in the highway. He
swerves quickly back into his lane.
Irate DRIVER passes Katrinka, shaking
his fist at Leo, who tries to refocus his
attention on the highway in front of him.
Instead he recalls a recent dream. FADE
to Leo in the front passenger seat and
Denise in the driver's seat of Katrinka. The motor is idling; the car's rear
wheels are just inches from the edge of
a sheer cliff.

                        LEO
            Put the gear in drive, then slowly
            step on the gas pedal.

Denise shifts gears and steps on the gas
pedal. Instead of going forward, Katrinka moves in reverse. Her rear wheels
balance dangerously on the edge of the
cliff.

                        LEO
                  (furious, panicked)
            What have you done? You've killed
            us both!

Katrinka tilts backwards and begins to
plummet down the cliff, first in slow motion, then gaining in momentum. Leo is
terrified, helpless, resigned. At the
apex of the convergence of all three
emotions, and with Katrinka in full free
fall, Leo embraces Denise and holds her
close.

The velocity is such that their bodies
are weightless.

                        LEO
                  (eyes closed, repeating like a
                  mantra)
            I love you, I love you, I love you,
            I love you…

As he continues to chant softly, Leo
no longer fears death. The car no longer plummets but decelerates, floating
as quietly and lightly as a snowflake.
What's more, Katrinka rights herself,
landing on all four wheels simultaneously at the moment of impact, at which
point LEO returns to reality, swerving
just in time to avoid hitting DOUGLAS,
walking on Cranston Road, who jumps onto
the sidewalk. Leo parks in the driveway
of his house, exits Katrinka and starts
climbing the ladder leaning against one
of the shorn sumac trees.

Margaret arrives and parks the Mercedes-Benz on the street. She, Denise,
and Lorraine see Leo and run to the
base of the sumac. Denise spies Douglas
across the street.

                    DENISE
               (yells)
          Douglas!

Douglas joins Denise, who is steadying the ladder. Worm's-eye view of Leo
climbing higher. The ladder trembles.

                    MARGARET
               (calls)
          Leo!

> LORRAINE

Daddy! Come down!

Worm's-eye view of Leo climbing higher
still. He slips on a rung, regains his
footing, and keeps climbing.

> DENISE
> (to DOUGLAS)

Stop him.

> DOUGLAS

What?

> DENISE
> (agitated)

My father. Stop him! He's going to
jump!

Denise starts to climb the ladder. Douglas nudges her aside and starts up the
ladder.

> DOUGLAS
> (to DENISE)

Hold it steady.

Lorraine joins Denise in steadying the
ladder, one on each side of it.

> MARGARET
> (supplicating)

Leo. Come back down. Please, Leo.

Having reached the top of the ladder,
Leo begins climbing up the tree branches
themselves.

> DOUGLAS
> (climbing faster)

Mr. Lin. Mr. Lin! Don't climb any
higher. The branches won't support
your weight.

Douglas climbs past the top of the ladder and onto some branches. Leo strad-
dles a fork between branches just above
Douglas.

> LEO
> (looking out over Cranston Road,
> to himself)

Funny. I'd never really noticed
what it looks like from up here.

> DOUGLAS

Mr. Lin, please come back down.
Your family is worried about you.

> LEO
> (noticing DOUGLAS for the first
> time)

Who are you? What are you doing in
my tree?

                    DOUGLAS
        Douglas. A friend of Denise. I'm a
        year ahead of her at Bronx Science.

                      LEO
              (offering his hand to shake)
        Hello, Douglas. I'm Denise's father.

                    DOUGLAS
              (hugging the tree trunk)
        Uh, I think you'd better hold onto
        the tree with that.

        LEO complies.

                      LEO
        Do you have a father?

                    DOUGLAS
                 (hesitantly)
        Ye-es.

                    MARGARET
                 (peering up)
        What in the world are they doing?

                      LEO
        What does he do? For a living.

                    DOUGLAS
        He's a trial lawyer.

                      LEO
        A good one?

                    DOUGLAS
          (shrugs)
You know. Wins some. Loses some.

                    LEO
And what do you want to be? A lawyer, like him?

                    DOUGLAS
I want to be a veterinarian. I
don't know what he'd like me to
be. He's never said. And he's never asked. I think he wants me to
decide for myself. When the time
comes. (laughs) And to be able to
support myself.

                    LEO
You have a good relationship with
him.

                    DOUGLAS
I dunno. (shrugs) Guess so. He's
the only father I've got. Right now
he's ticked off at me.

                    LEO
Why?

                    DOUGLAS
I filched some of his cigarettes.

                    LEO
Dunhills.

                    DOUGLAS
          (amazed)
How'd you know what brand he
smokes?

                    LEO
Lucky guess.

                    DOUGLAS
Did he blow his top! When he found
out, he…

                    LEO
Made you smoke the whole pack.

                    DOUGLAS
          (stupefied)
How did you…?

                    LEO
Another lucky guess.

                    DOUGLAS
          (catching on)
Oh. (chuckles) Poor Denise! That's
funny.

                    LEO
What is?

                              DOUGLAS
That you and my dad had the same
idea. That you and I are sitting up
in this tree talking. And that Denise was afraid you were going to
jump.

Leo looks down at his family below.
Bird's-eye view of Margaret, Denise, and
Lorraine looking anxiously up at him.

                              DOUGLAS
                           (dubiously)

You weren't thinking of jumping,
were you. Mr. Lin. WERE you?

Nai-nai appears at the attic window,
one of Guoxin's vertical scrolls in her
hands. She looks pointedly at Leo and
unfurls it. It is of a deciduous tree
half of whose leaves lie at the base of
its trunk. The border and the calligraphy
are in gold leaf. The calligraphy reads:
NO MATTER HOW HIGH THE TREE GROWS, THE
LEAVES FALL BACK TO ITS ROOTS.
C.U. of the epiphanic, poignant expression on Leo's face.

INT. LIN MASTER BEDROOM — HALF AN HOUR LATER

      MARGARET
     (on the phone)
  I have to see you. It can't wait.
  (pause) No, he's here. Speaking
  with his mother. In the guest room.

INT. LIN HOUSE KITCHEN

  C.U. of Leo on the phone listering in on
  Margaret's conversation.

      MARGARET (O.S.)
  Something's happened. Something important. I can drive up right now.
  Right this minute. Okay. See you
  soon.

  CLICK of the receiver. DIAL TONE. Leo
  hangs up.

INT. DENISE AND LORRAINE'S BEDROOM

  Denise and Lorraine are lolling on their
  beds, pretending to read.

      LORRAINE
  Den.

      DENISE
  Uhm.

                    LORRAINE

So… Do you think Daddy wanted to
kill himself?

                    DENISE

Don't be silly. He just wanted to
get away from it all. Where else
could he go? Besides, you can't
kill yourself jumping from a height
of three stories.

                    LORRAINE

Sure you can — if you land on your
head and break your neck.

                    DENISE
        (irked)

Or he could've broken his back and
spent the rest of his life in a
wheelchair. Gee whizz, Rainey!

                    LORRAINE

So… What do you think he's doing
now?

                    DENISE

Planning his next suicide attempt.

                    LORRAINE

Stop it!

                    DENISE

Didn't you hear what he said? He
wanted to get away from it all. He
wanted to get away from US. Didn't
you see the suitcases outside the
guest room door?

They hear a KNOCK on the door. Margaret
opens it part-way.

                    MARGARET

I need to pick up a few things at
Freddie's Corner before it closes.
I'll see you both later. (closes
the door)

                    DENISE
             (bounding off her bed)

No, you're right. We should be
watching him. Just in case. C'mon.

INT. OUTSIDE GUEST ROOM DOOR — MOMENTS LATER

Margaret approaches the closed door,
glances at Leo's luggage outside it.
Hesitates, then knocks gently.

                    MARGARET
             (through closed door)

Leo. (silence) I have to go to the
pharmacy. If I don't see you when I
get back… (wavery voice) Good-bye.

Margaret exits through the back door.

INT. GUEST ROOM

The room is empty. Leo is gone. PAN to
OPEN WINDOW where Denise and Lorraine
peer inside over the window ledge.

EXT. CRANSTON ROAD OUTSIDE LIN HOUSE

Margaret gets into Evelyn's Mercedes-Benz. Nai-nai, in her front yard
vegetable garden, watches her drive off.

EXT. LIN DRIVEWAY

Leo sits at the wheel of Katrinka. Seeing Margaret drive off, he starts the
motor. Denise and Lorraine open the back
doors and get inside.

> LEO
> (startled)

What…?! Get out!

> LORRAINE

You can't make us.

> LEO

You're staying home. Both of you.

> DENISE

We're going with you, like it or not.
(points) Look! She's getting away!

LEO
(shifts into reverse)

All right. You asked for it.

Leo backs down the driveway and follows Margaret.

EXT. A GINGERBREAD COTTAGE IN THE COUNTRY — HALF AN HOUR LATER

Margaret parks the Mercedes in front of the cottage, walks up the front steps and enters. Seconds later, Leo drives up in Katrinka

LEO

The perfect love nest. (to DENISE and LORRAINE) I warned you. You're not going to like what you see.

They enter the cottage and see Margaret, Prudie, and Mark standing in the kitchen. A moment of STUNNED SILENCE.

LORRAINE
(ecstatic)

Prudie!

Leo grabs Lorraine to prevent her from running to Prudie.

                         PRUDIE
                (straining for composure)
          Daddy, I'd like you to meet Mark.
          My husband.

                         MARK
                (approaches LEO and extends his
                hand)
          Mr. Lin.

          Leo just stares at him. Mark drops his
          hand to his side.

                         PRUDIE
          Den. Rainey. This is Mark. Mark, my
          sisters Denise and Lorraine.

                         DENISE
                (between shyness and suspicion)
          Hi.

          Lorraine looks at Mark with curiosity,
          then smiles.

                         MARK
          I've heard a lot about you both. I hope
          to get to know you better. In time.

                         LORRAINE
                (presses close to MARGARET;
                whispers)
          That's Prudie's husband?

          Denise gives Lorraine a dirty look.

MARK

Prudie, maybe we can put the kettle
on for tea or…

LEO
(abrupt)

We just ate. (looks around) This is
where you live?

MARK

Well, the cottage is ours. Prudie's and mine. But yes, it's a family business. My granddad started it forty years ago. It's grown
a lot since then. (spritely) "Happy
Hollow Farm and Nursery. For the
green thumb in you."

LEO

And what do you do here?

MARK

Whatever needs doing. Sales. Or-
dering supplies. Planting. Weeding.
Fertilizing. Sprouting. Pruning.

LEO

Pruning.

MARK

Trees. Pruning trees. I'm a certi-
fied tree surgeon. As of almost two
months ago.

                         LEO
                    (whips out his hand; MARK
                    shakes it)
          Leo Lin. Prudie's father. I take
          it (meaningfully) that you already
          know my… Margaret (to MARGARET)
          Those nights when you had to work
          late…

                         MARGARET
          I was here. Mark picked me up in
          the city. Most of those nights. Not
          all of them. Once in a while, I did
          have to work late.

                         PRUDIE
          When we could, Mark and I — some-
          times just me — would come into
          town and have lunch with Mom at
          that little…

                         LEO
          Luncheonette. On Madison. Two
          blocks from St. Patrick's. (looks
          at MARGARET) You. You were having
          lunch. With Prudie.

                         MARGARET
          That man. Behind the lamppost
          across the street. In the fedora
          and dark glasses.

          That was YOU!

Bewildered, Denise and Lorraine stare at
Leo.

> LEO
> (embarrassed, brusquely to
> DENISE and LORRAINE)

You two. We're going home.

> LORRAINE

I'm staying. (clings to MARGARET)
I'm going home with Mom.

> LEO

Denise?

> DENISE
> (reluctant)

I…

> PRUDIE

Before any of you leave, now that
everyone's here, Mark and I have an
announcement to make. We're going
to be married. And we'd like you
all to come to the wedding.

> MARGARET

I thought you were already married.

> PRUDIE

At City Hall. Now we want to get
married with all the trimmings
(takes MARK'S hand) in a religious
ceremony.

                         MARGARET
                    (ecstatic)

          Oh, Prudie! If there was one wish
          I had for you…

                         PRUDIE

          Mom.

                         MARGARET

          …it was that you would marry in St.
          Agatha's. With masses of flowers and
          white candles on the altar…

                         PRUDIE

          Mom. Mark and I want to be married
          — in a Jewish ceremony.

The muscles of Margaret's face slack-
en. Her eyes express shock and disbelief.
She lowers herself into a chair.

                         MARK
                    (quickly)

          Reformed. My family's reformed.
          We're not orthodox. Never have been.

                         PRUDIE
                    (kneeling at MARGARET'S side)

          I've been studying with a rabbi
          ever since Mark asked me to marry
          him. I'm converting to Judaism.

Margaret stares at Prudie as though
she's seeing a stranger — worse, as if

she's been betrayed by her first-born.

> PRUDIE
>
> I know this is a surprise — a shock
> — to you. But I've thought it over
> carefully, since it was my idea —
> not Mark's — in the first place. Ac-
> tually, I had to convince him. So
> this is the decision we've made.
> Together. It's what we think is
> best for us. And for the children
> we plan to have, eventually. (takes
> MARGARET'S hand in hers) I want
> Mark and me to be a united front.
> In everything. In love. In marriage.
> In raising our family.

> MARK
> (to MARGARET)
>
> I think what Prudie is trying
> to say is — do you give us your
> blessing?

Margaret is silent. Mark turns to Leo.

> MARK
>
> Mr. Lin?

> LEO
>
> Leo.

> MARK
>
> Do you give us your blessing… Leo?

C.U. of Denise struggling not to cry.

                    LEO
          (looks from DENISE to LORRAINE
          to MARK and PRUDIE)
      I do.

Leo looks at Margaret, tears welling up
in her eyes.

                    PRUDIE
      Mom?

                    LEO
      Margaret?

Margaret looks up at Leo.
WHITE LETTERS ON A BLACK SCREEN. THE WORDS
APPEAR SEQUENTIALLY, AS IF SOMEONE IS WRIT-
ING THEM BY HAND, LETTER BY LETTER.

There's no vocabulary

For love within a family, love that's
lived in

But not looked at, love within the light
of which

All else is seen, the love within which

All other love finds speech. This love
is silent.

— T.S. Eliot

Acknowledgments

Many people have kept me company one way or another in the solitary process of writing this book made more solitary by the Covid pandemic. I am deeply indebted to Diane Goettel for her thoughtful and thorough editing and, together with her colleagues at Black Lawrence Press, for guiding *The Forest for the Trees* from manuscript to finished book. I am most grateful, first and foremost, to my Ba-Li Fami-Li for their love, support and shared mealtimes, especially Amazing Grace, who gives me hope beyond hope. To my friends throughout the years: Kathryn Kass, Solange Ferré, Pamela Frasca, Barbara Daelman, Julia Zanes, Hilary Blake, Patricia Dodd, Jeannie Weatherbee, Robin Glazer, Michelle Repiso, Christa Uebel, Jane Leung Larson, Stella Dong, Kathy Wah Lee, Gwynne Tuan, Ruth Ulferts, John Rayner, and Amy and Cameron Middleton. And to Patricia Fraser and Edgar Milford who offered me respite, repose, and encouragement when I sorely needed them. And last and far from least, to DMMD.

Leslie Li is the author of *Bittersweet: A Novel*, *Daughter of Heaven: A Memoir with Earthly Recipes*, and *Just Us Girls*, the companion book to her feature-length documentary *The Kim Loo Sisters*. She is the recipient of the Big Moose Prize for Fiction and Tennessee Williams Scholarship in Fiction as well as grants from New York State Council for the Arts, Lower Manhattan Cultural Council, and Chinese Heritage Foundation. Her personal essays and feature articles have appeared in The *New York Times*, *The Christian Science Monitor*, *Travel & Leisure*, *Condé Nast Traveler*, *Gourmet*, *Saveur*, *Garden Design*, *Modern Maturity*, *Dorothy Parker's Ashes*, and elsewhere. *Bittersweet* and *Daughter of Heaven* have been translated into five languages. She lives in New York.